Theta Corps

RESTITUTION

ALIYAH BURKE

Restitution
ISBN # 978-1-78686-320-1
©Copyright Aliyah Burke 2017
Cover Art by Posh Gosh ©Copyright September 2017
Interior text design by Claire Siemaszkiewicz
Totally Bound Publishing

Published in 2017 by Totally Bound Publishing, Think Tank, Ruston Way, Lincoln, LN6 7FL, United Kingdom.

RESTITUTION

Dedication

Thanks to all my readers who've waited for the Theta Corps series to come out. I hope you enjoy them all. Thanks to my editor for helping me make it shine and to Totally Bound for taking another series from me. DH, I love you and couldn't do this without you.

Chapter One

Retribution – requital according to merits or deserts, especially for evil.

The *plip* of water, annoying as it may be, beside his head was the ongoing reminder he still lived. The radiating pain coursing through him was the other aide-mémoire he breathed. It was excruciating to complete the simple task. Calling his situation 'alive' fell into the 'it's a stretch' category.

Ethan Jackson had gone and gotten himself into one hell of a situation.

Rats crawled along his feet and up his legs, biting when and where they chose. He didn't move. There was no point in expending his limited energy in a major attempt to knock the vermin off when they'd just climb back on. Time had long since lost all meaning for him. Other than pain, pretty much everything had. He struggled to remember the faces of his sister and cousin. And his own name.

Heavy footsteps clomped along the damp concrete hall. Every few paces — three — the foot splashed into a puddle. He tensed — either he was losing more time or they were coming back to torture him once more.

Muffled voices reached him as the footsteps stopped. He waited for the door to open, anxious for the tiniest shaft of grimy light to penetrate his world of darkness. After a period of his own warring uncertainty, he noted the footsteps move on. He closed his eyes and attempted to get more rest.

He'd seen the rows of doors each time they'd dragged him to a better-lit room to torture him. He was unsure, however, if there were actual people behind them. Screams — other than his — came occasionally but he'd yet to see another who was being treated in the same vein as him and hadn't given in to the belief there were more prisoners here.

Wherever the fuck I am.

All he recalled with positive clarity was Virginia had been his last definitive location. However, again, that was where the time issue came back into play. He had no knowledge of how long he'd been a prisoner. His struggle to remain alert and strong was more than enough of a challenge. With the rotten food and putrid water, there wasn't much in the way to sustain mental acuity or physical prowess.

The footsteps returned and he forced himself to remain still and not tense.

"Get up!"

He opened his eyes in time to see Hitler's poster boys standing over him and one deliver a powerful kick to his ribs. Movement was slow — no one wanted to hurry to their next bout of torture.

Ethan didn't help much, aware they would drag him up and out of the tiny cell. Sure, his knees got the brunt of it but he conserved energy. True to form, they swore at him in German before yanking him up by his armpits.

All y'all are going to die. I will not *die in this cesspool. I'll escape and kill each of you for what you've done to me.* His mantra played on a continuous loop in his mind. It offered the slightest bit of hope to his situation.

They dragged him from the cell, his legs sliding over water and other substances he didn't want to think about. He eyed the heavy black boots the two men had, wishing they were on his feet. His own shoes were long gone.

A stone door opened and they entered. Squinting from the light, he gazed around the room. Ethan recognized the man who implemented the torture. His gray linen suit perfectly pressed. Then again, it always was…at the start.

This time there was another in the room. Thin and clad in torn clothing, a black girl stood there holding a tray of something he couldn't see. Not that he wanted to know what it held.

"Mr. Jackson," the man said in a quiet authoritative tone, sliding off his suit coat. "This is going to be our last meeting." He unbuttoned and rolled up his sleeves, the gray vest perfect against his crisp white shirt. "You have been a most amazing volunteer. Your ability to withhold your cries of pain has made you somewhat of a legend."

He pulled on the bottom of his vest. "I wonder if your sister will last as long once she's in my chair. Will her screams be full-bodied or sharp and high? I want to find out. I shudder with anticipation." He grinned. "I will leave you to them. They want to inflict pain on you and we have so few joys out here in the rainforest."

Ethan's blood turned to ice at the mention of his sister. Rage poured into him as if someone had opened the floodgates. He struggled to remain impassive. Internally, however, he killed the German he knew only as Rolf, very meticulous and slow, not to mention with excruciating pain.

He lifted his gaze and focused on the female. She held his gaze, dropping hers to stare at the floor. *I'm in the rainforest.*

"Put him in the chair." The order was barked in German.

Tweedledum and Tweedledee shoved him in the chair then held his arms. He glared at the man who neared, memorizing him so he would be able to find him in the future and kill him. An alarm blared and Rolf pivoted.

"Goddamn locals!" He ran to the door, the two goons following, slammed it shut, locking Ethan in with the woman.

Ethan held himself immobile for a tense moment. Was it a trick? He darted his gaze to her. She continued to stand in the far corner, eyes still on the floor, as if trying to make herself as small as she could or invisible.

He pushed up from the wooden chair, his attention split between her — who appeared a bit older than he'd first believed — and the door. Now that he was upright, he saw some syringes on the tray.

One step toward her then the door crashed open, allowing the Hitler poster boy to barrel into the small cell. Ethan didn't hesitate, just lunged at him and brought him down, digging his ragged nails into the man's eye sockets. While it took him longer than it should have to overpower and kill him, he soon stood, victorious. Blood dripped from his fingers.

He peeked back to the woman on the side. She hadn't moved.

"Come here," he snapped, wiping the blood from his mouth with the back of his hand before he patted down the dead man.

She didn't move.

He ordered her again in German. She lifted her head and sighed softly then shuffled toward him. Her steps were slow, as if she bore some unseen shackles on her thin legs, but her speed—little that it was—remained constant. Ethan took the syringes, checked to make sure they were capped and put them in his pocket. Then he removed the boots and socks of his jailer.

The entire time, alarms blared and she stood like a statue.

"Come," he barked in German.

Again, she listened but he noted her hesitation. He yanked the tray from her hands and tossed it away. Her body jerked and trembled.

What kind of man leaves a woman in with a prisoner? Either she's expendable or the racist fuck trusts her.

He snaked his arm around her neck, grateful his fingers were around the man's assault rifle. He held the side arm in the hand by her throat. "You're my ticket out. Where's the exit? And I will kill you first if you lead me to a trap."

Her body never stopped trembling as she pointed down the darkened passageway. In the back of his mind, he could hear his grandmother's mental reprimand about how wrong it was to treat women in such a fashion. He pressed the muzzle against the junction of her neck and shoulder.

"Don't test me," he commanded in guttural German.

His prisoner never spoke a word as she pointed him to his freedom. Tense, exhausted, he remained alert when they came to a dead end.

He growled under his breath. "I warned you."

She pointed up and he followed with his gaze. A hatch along the wall with a rough ladder built into it.

Ethan pushed his exhaustion to the back of his mind. "We're about to get all kinds of personal. Same rules apply." He shouldered the rifle, pushed her toward the ladder. Shoving the handgun in the front of his nearly destroyed pants, he pressed against her. "You climb with me. Don't be stupid."

Still nothing verbal from her. She reached out and began to climb. He mimicked her, keeping her tight between him and the ladder. At the top, she halted and he reached over her to open the hatch, inch by inch.

Blue sky dotted with white clouds had him squinting as tears sprang to his eyes. After months of near darkness, this sliver of real light bordered on painful. He nudged her up one more step. It wasn't pretty but he got them out.

One hand around her mouth, he closed the door, his gaze darting around. Backing away, toward the thick waiting rainforest, he moved them from the groomed area of the compound.

Voices had him dropping flat to the ground, eyes locked with his hostage, the barrel of the Desert Eagle by her chest between her breasts. No anger was in her eyes, only acceptance of whatever he decided to mete out to her. It rubbed him wrong.

She held his gaze and barely blinked as two men passed by. *Perhaps she's not working with them.* He had a hard time believing these arrogant replicas of the Third Reich would employ—much less trust—a black woman. He moved without delay as the men continued on. *Not very thorough with alarms going off.*

Ethan breathed easier when the rainforest swallowed him up. At least now he had a chance. More alarms blared and he realized his escape had been noted.

A feral grin crossed his face. Time for some payback. He turned to the woman. He ran his gaze over her then around. Stepping away, he took hold of some vines.

"Against the tree."

She didn't argue and he roped her tight with as much speed as he could. Patting his pocket to ensure the syringes were there, he met her gaze. "Keep quiet and I'll come back and cut you free. I have no designs to hurt you if you follow what I say. You help them and I'll kill you as well."

Again, not so much as a sigh. She'd resigned herself to her fate. There went that damn niggling again. He tapped the gun against his cheek as he backed away. He had some men to kill then a home with a life to return to.

* * * *

"Wake up, Mino."

"This better be a damn good reason for you to be in my bedroom, Beauregard."

He kicked her bed frame with one booted foot as he turned on a light. "Come on."

"You breaking into my home is a bit much, don't you think?"

"It wasn't hard. Your security system sucks." Beau stared at the woman glaring at him. Her gaze raked over him before it narrowed.

"You'd better not be bleeding on my floor."

He didn't pause or look to his newest injury. "I need you to take out a bullet."

She tossed back the blankets and slid from her double bed. "They have hospitals, you know. Places where trained people wait to do those kinds of things." She planted her hands on her hips clad in Wonder Woman images and symbols. *Never knew she was into Wonder Woman.*

She yawned. "They even have the proper equipment. Then you wouldn't have sauntered into my dreams."

He lifted an eyebrow.

She held out a hand and waved it at him. "Not what I meant, because I wasn't indicating you were in my dreams. I meant because you interrupted my dreams and—oh, never mind. Let's get this over with so I can go back to sleep."

He trailed her into the small bathroom where he sat on her counter then drew off his shirt.

"You know I'm not a doctor." She removed her eye mask and wasted no time putting her hair up in a ponytail.

"You were in med school." Her gaze snapped to him. "I checked you out. You did three years before—shit!" He jerked his head to where she'd poked his injury. "That hurt."

"My personal life is off limits."

You don't have a personal life. You were sleeping alone on a Friday night. He kept that to himself as she poked and prodded to get out the bullet.

"If you look like this, what do the others look like?"

"Worse."

She grunted. "I won't lie to Masters when he asks."

"I'll be gone by then."

She paused, moving back to peer at him. "You have word on Ethan?"

He stared in her eyes. "Yes."

Mino held his gaze then returned to his injury. "Where is he?"

"Venezuela." Aside from a select few, he'd not shared that with anyone. Mino was one of theirs. Personal secretary to his boss. Someone who had no problem helping them out. But she answered to Masters.

"When do you leave?"

"Soon."

She turned and walked to her bedroom, removing the gloves as she did so. He hopped off and followed, hand over his still-open wound. She was shoving items in a bag.

"What are you doing? I need you to finish this."

She tugged a sweatshirt on then removed the blue cami she'd been wearing, tossing it into a wicker hamper in the corner. "Packing."

"I gathered that," he drawled. "Why?"

After putting on a bra, she shucked her shorts, exchanging them for some hot pink lounge pants. "To go."

"Hell no. You're not coming."

She snorted and grabbed another pack that she checked before nodding sharply. "Let's go. I'll patch you up on the flight."

He took her upper arm as she tried to move by him, one bag over her shoulder and a duffel in the other. "You're *not* going."

"Yes. I am. Let's go." Defiance sparked in her light-brown eyes.

"I'm not taking care of you in the rainforest."

"Ethan—"

"May not even recognize me."

"He may not but chances are he *will* most likely need medical attention. What were you planning on doing, taking him to the local hospital?" She jerked free of his touch and left the room. She cleaned up her bathroom and waited for him by the door.

Damn. She was right.

* * * *

Splash! The cold water made her sputter and cough as it flowed past her face. She struggled to open her eyes, but the left was swollen shut.

Rally squinted through her one useable eye. The ropes hanging her dug into her wrists. Her feet dangled over the ground.

In front of her stood the man who called himself Rolf. Not his real name — she knew that — but it was what he went by. His dark-blond brows slashed forward in disappointment.

"Rally, Rally, Rally. You know this upsets me. I thought we had an understanding. You don't leave. And yet" — he unfurled the long bullwhip, dragging the studded tips over the dirty ground — "my men caught you out in the rainforest."

Tied to a damn tree but that never mattered to Rolf. He wanted to make her bleed. And she would.

"I house you. Feed you. Clothe you. And you behave in such a manner." His words were laced with anger.

Despite the expectation of what was coming, the first lash never failed to shock her. By the third, her dress lay below her feet. She closed her eyes, the tears burning to fall.

I may cry but he'll never get me to cry out.

"Where did he go?" Rolf demanded.

She hadn't any clue. Not that she'd tell if she did. He seemed to understand and the whip flashed over and over until she fell into a world of darkness where the agony was held at bay.

When she woke she gasped as the pain tore through her. The camp was dark, the silence broken by the occasional scream of an animal and ones of women.

She wriggled her fingers as a fire owned her. Back, legs, every inch was aflame. Keeping mute, she waited, knowing what was coming.

"Someday, you won't defy me." The glow of his cigarette broke the darkness before a flashlight clicked on, blinding her. She averted her eyes.

He touched her cheek and she steeled against his touch.

"Things would be much easier if you would just—" He sighed. "I've tried over and over to show you how it could be for us. You continue to run. I spared you."

More tears gathered as he touched the fresh welts.

"Cut her down. Take her to my room." Disappointment rang in his tone.

A whimper escaped when two men removed her without any caution before dragging her back to her feet. One then tossed her naked body over his shoulder.

"Don't bleed on me, bitch," he snapped.

A small woman waited in Rolf's lit quarters. Dumped on the tick bedding upon the floor, she lay on her belly, waiting for her wounds to be cleaned. All ritual. The woman wasn't gentle and Rally bit her lip to keep from screaming.

When she was alone and clothed, she clumsily drew a blanket over her body, grateful to be in a dress instead of naked, no matter how ragged it was.

The next day, she moved slower than usual because of her back and returned to her list of tasks. Along one edge of the village in view of the guards, she worked the pile of dishes she had to finish.

A shout came from the left and she ignored it. Nothing good came from being nosy. The cry was followed by an explosion that took her to her knees, the tub of water capsizing, dumping all its contents.

She remained flat, the water soaking her. It had happened before, the attacks. She'd learned long ago it was best to stay down until the commotion stopped.

A rough hand grabbed her around the wrist, yanking hard. She blinked away more tears to focus on the scowling face of Rolf's sadistic right-hand man.

"Come on, whore."

She was forced to run after him, his steps were so large. Her wounds tore open and she blinked away her tears. He secured her to a pole. One she'd seen him use when he forced himself on a woman.

"Rolf is blinded by you." He grabbed her chin and pain shot through her. "I will use you then dispose of you. You've been quiet through everything but I *will* make you scream." He shoved her away from him and she hit the pole hard, stars exploding before her eyes.

He left. Time passed as she remained unable to move.

A noise behind her had her peering painfully over her shoulder. *What is* he *doing here?* The prisoner, Ethan Jackson, stepped into view. His gaunt features didn't distract from the dangerous aura surrounding him. In fact, it may have enhanced it.

Their eyes locked and he whipped out a large knife. *Did he come to kill me?*

He sliced through the ropes at her wrist.

"Come."

She ignored the outstretched hand and moved on her own. Pain meant she had survived another day. He didn't respond to her slight of avoiding him.

"Where is he?" He stepped up to her before rooting through the clothing there.

She longed to grab another shirt but remained immobile. *I'm not certain he's not still going to kill me.* Ethan stood with new clothes in hand. He ripped off the torn shirt and drew on the dark-brown one. Up his side, she noticed a tattooed phrase.

Latin. *Semper en Obscurus.* Always in the dark. She lowered her gaze and backed up a step.

He had a weapon pointed at her. "No moving. And I asked you a question. Is that bastard here?" He undid his torn pants and kicked free of them before drawing on the clean pair. "Do you understand me? I want the man called Rolf. Is he here?"

She shook her head.

He fastened the pants and set the gun down to add a belt. Then he put on socks and boots. "No, he's not here? Or no, you don't understand me?"

Rally flexed her fingers and stared at the ground.

"I'm betting you don't want to talk to me but you understand. Nod if you meant that jackass Rolf isn't in camp."

She nodded as he strapped holsters to each leg, seeming more dangerous than before. Despite being so thin after his imprisonment, with hair reaching his shoulders and the beard, he appeared wild and untamed. His brown eyes constantly were on the move.

He bent and tossed her another shirt. "Let's go."

She caught it out of reflex, more tears stinging her eyes. *He's taking me?* A whimper escaped as she tried to draw the shirt over her head.

"Are you hurt? Aside from the bruise on your face?"

If I say yes, he may leave me. Her decision came too slow for his apparent liking and he strode to her side.

"Turn around."

Her hopes sinking, she turned. She remained like a tree as he ripped through the dress. "Who did this to you?" His question vibrated with anger. "Was it the asshole who had you tied up in here?"

She gave a slow shake of her head.

"Rolf?"

A nod this time. The muggy air stuck to her skin.

He moved to her front and assisted her on with the new shirt then got her a pair of pants that had to be tied on.

"Let's go."

Rally didn't hesitate but followed him out into the compound and on through to the waiting rainforest. She locked her own pain away and hurried to keep up. He stopped so abruptly she nearly ran into his back.

He pivoted. "Walk ahead of me."

With him behind her, they progressed farther from camp and deeper into the forest. Sweat ran down her back, stinging the injuries with the salt.

"Stop."

Her feet riveted to the spot, fear he would kill her because was slowing him up too much, almost freezing her. Yet still she turned to look at him. Sweat streamed down his face as well and he'd lost what little color he had. She took a gaze about and picked a spot. Reaching for his arm, she tugged on him.

He stumbled with her and she got him behind a large, moss-covered felled tree. She checked and rechecked to be confident no one was right behind them.

He didn't look good. At all.

Scanning the large-leafed trees, she saw what she needed to get. He watched her, bringing up the weapon when she stepped back. Rally held out her hands before pointing toward the treetops.

"Stay here."

She shook her head and pointed again, then moved determinedly. Smothering her own discomfort, she vanished into the branches. She checked the large leaves until she located one with water. Moving cautiously, she attempted to break off the leaf while keeping the liquid there. It didn't work and she swore as it spilled, falling away.

Rally huffed in frustration and pain. She found another and tipped the leaf to her mouth, allowing the water to roll in. Two more leaves and she had a mouthful.

Then began her arduous journey down. When she had to swallow, she bent her head down and pushed the liquid as far forward as she could then took as little water as she could.

She hurried over the thick moss until she reached Ethan. His eyes flicked open as the pistol in his hand lifted.

"I thought you left me."

She knelt beside him with a shake of her head. *How do I do this?* She inched closer before bumping his thigh. His weapon remained in hand and he put the muzzle to her chest as she cupped his face, his beard abrading her palms. She tilted her head and kissed him.

Chapter Two

Ethan blinked twice, dropped his gun, and accepted the slow stream of water she pushed into his mouth. Greedy, he sucked it down, not realizing how thirsty he'd been. When she began to move away, he grabbed the back of her head, anchoring them together. She pushed on his shoulders and he released her. Her eyes were dark and she pointed back up. Then she was gone.

His silent companion took ten more trips before his thirst had been marginally quenched. On the last time, he sat up, cupped her head, wanting her closer. He may have been hurt but she was a woman and he hadn't had one in a long time. As she had with her other trips, the moment the water had been passed, she backed away.

He held her wrist when she attempted to push to her feet. "Rest," he said.

She shook her head and pointed to his left. He peered in that direction. More thick foliage. "You want to go there?"

At her affirmative nod, he rose, the water having helped a lot.

"Lead on."

She'd won his trust. He watched her move over the ground. Even with her injuries, she had a grace about her. Every so often she paused and changed directions. It continued until the sun was about to set. There was a tall rock wall covered with numerous twisted greenery. She approached and moved some aside, showing a small cutout.

He turned to face the direction they'd come. A perfect vantage point. Ethan moved to stand before her. Lifting her chin, he kissed her. His intent to keep it simple. A thank-you. He realized he was in trouble when he slipped his tongue into her mouth.

He stumbled away and her eyes grew wide. "Thank you," he muttered. She turned, placing some large leaves by the entrance.

They settled in, backs to the stone wall. With the foliage over the opening, it was black inside. He reached out for her then tugged on her until she came closer.

"I know you're in pain but sit here." He repositioned her between his legs, so she wasn't against the rock wall. "I won't hurt you. Rest. We'll share heat."

He dozed on and off through the night, her slim figure to him the entire time. Her stirring woke him and she moved away, stiff. He rose with her and peered out through the vines. Nothing looked out of the ordinary.

She pushed out and crouched by what she'd set up the previous night. He glanced down. She'd collected water. He took it from her when she offered and drank, pausing before he finished.

"Did you have some?"

She cut her eyes to the right then nodded. He knew that second she lied. He tipped it up then put the leaf down. When she stood and began to move by him, he stopped her. "We'll go get you some water now."

Her nod was timid.

Capturing her hand, he set off not willing to give up the first non-painful human contact in longer than he cared to remember. If he made her uncomfortable, she didn't fight him on it.

They continued away from his prison. *Hers too, from the looks of how she was treated.*

They came across a small stream that cut through. Each sank to their knees and gulped the fresh, clear liquid. He scooped up handfuls to splash on his neck. His bushy beard and stringy hair felt a tiny bit better after he soaked them.

He heard it the same time she scrambled to her feet. There was no mistaking the heavy clomp of boots through underbrush. Especially when those approaching didn't care how much noise they stirred up.

"Hide," he whispered roughly.

Before she moved, gunfire broke out and he flattened, indicating she do the same. She did and he leaped on the first man who crashed through the tall grass.

One of the guys from camp. Ethan wrestled him, hissing in pain as the knife sank in his skin. The gun went off by his ear, setting off a ringing in his skull. He buried the blade in the man's neck. Rolling free, he palmed the pistol then shot the next man.

He scrambled to her, yanking her up. "Move!"

She stumbled and he latched on to her arm, keeping her upright. The next two he shot as well. His body shook with exhaustion, and when the pistol was empty, he dropped it, pulling another.

They couldn't move fast enough and the gunfire faded. He kept her behind him and stared with defiance at the two men surrounding them.

"I'm going to kill you," one man sneered seconds before his head exploded. The other had no time to comprehend anything as his brain matter joined the first guy's.

She clutched the back of his shirt, trembling.

"Ethan?"

He gulped and drew another gun. He had to be hallucinating for he swore he heard his sister's voice.

"Ethan?"

She stepped into view. Dressed in jungle camo, her vibrant red hair in a braid over one shoulder and a black skullcap on top. She carried a Kalashnikov in her left hand.

"Do you see a redhead?" he whispered in German to the woman standing off to the side behind him. He watched for her response in his periphery.

He was malnourished. No telling what hallucinations he was experiencing. Her nod had him blinking back tears. She'd arrived.

"Anabelle Lee?"

She ran toward him as two others stepped into view. He lifted the guns.

"Oh my God, I thought I'd lost you. *We* thought we'd lost you, but we refused to give up." She ignored his weapons and plastered kisses on his face, her own shiny with tears.

"Let the man breathe."

She released him and he noticed his cousin Beauregard there, looking ready to take on an army by himself. Valentino Cassano was behind him and at his side was another woman. He'd never seen a more perfect sight.

"Hate to break it up but we need to move," Valentino stated.

The woman approached and he blinked before recognition hit him. "Mino?"

She smiled and nodded. He noticed the tears in her eyes. "Are you okay to get to the chopper or do you need something now?"

"Got any morphine in there?"

"Always."

God, he loved her. "I'll make it. They may have carried me in here, but I'm damn well walking out. However, *she* may need something." He drew his silent companion out from behind him.

"Shit," Beauregard growled. "Who's this?"

"Don't know. She's not spoken a word. All I know is she saved my life and I'm not leaving her here. They whipped her and beat her." Tipping his head to meet her worried gaze, he asked, "Can you keep going? Once we get you to the chopper, we'll figure out who you are."

He'd expected another nod, not the blatant panic that surged across her features, seconds before she bolted, heading right back to where they'd come from.

"The fuck?"

She was quick but his sister was faster. Anabelle had her by the hair and yanked her back. The woman wouldn't hold still and just continued to struggle until Mino stabbed her in the arm with something. Her opposition ceased as she collapsed into a pile.

"Let's move," Beauregard said in his thick drawl, moving to the unconscious woman's side and slinging her over his shoulder like a bag of grain.

Ethan wanted to carry her but he knew he was going to be pushing it to make it back himself. They all began the trek. Mino remained near him, keeping an eye on him. Yes, he accepted he needed attention but it would wait until they were in the air. When he could relax.

The sun had begun to set when they entered another clearing. Val whistled and moments later Ethan heard the sound of an engine warming up. They rounded a small outcrop of trees and he saw the bird waiting for them.

"Welcome home," Giovanni, Val's brother, said as he opened the side door.

"Thanks." Ethan's body shook from exhaustion and he took the assistance to make it inside the helicopter.

"Sit," Mino said as she climbed up beside him.

He didn't fuss when she hooked him up to an IV and proceeded to check him out the rest of the way. His gaze, however, remained on the woman still knocked out.

"We need to run her prints and find out who she is," Val said as Gio got them airborne.

"No," Ethan barked, earning surprised looks from everyone. "She didn't want that to happen so she must have a reason. She'll tell me."

"You said she'd not spoken to you at all."

"But she did save my life when it would have been so easy for her to go off and leave me. In fact, Mino, take a look at her back and make sure it's not infected."

She rose and went to the woman's side. "Fuck," she swore as she turned her and lifted the shirt. "I hope to God you killed who did this to her."

"Not yet, but I will." It was a vow. A promise. His word. Anabelle sat beside him and took his hand. He squeezed her fingers, knowing how it had affected her.

He closed his eyes and drifted off to sleep, the familiar *whomp* of the helicopter soothing. He was going home. *Finally.*

* * * *

Rally woke with a start. She opened her eyes and looked around. Nothing was familiar to her. Light pushed away the darkness. Bright. Unfiltered. *Where am I?*

The panic began to set in as memories flashed. Other people. Ones she didn't know. But *he* had. Then they'd chased her and drugged her. Had she gone from her hell to a deeper level?

Tense, she gingerly sat. Soft golds and creams accented the darker brown in the room. A window on either side of the room brought in the light. Was she moving? She couldn't be positive for she was still groggy.

Rally smoothed her fingers along the satin comforter. How long had it been since she'd felt anything like this? Across from her was a brown couch with accent pillows the same color as the one on her side. Tears pricked her eyes and she turned to look out of the window.

Shit. I'm on a plane? Where could they possibly be taking me? Not back there?

A knock preceded a woman sticking her head in. She gave a slight smile, perfect teeth shining from her mocha skin.

"Good, you're awake. Mind if I come in?" She entered without waiting for a response.

Rally averted her eyes. It had been a long time since she'd heard English, aside from the man who'd saved her. The one she'd come to know as Ethan Jackson.

"So, I need to check your back and put some more salve on your cuts. On your stomach, please." She made a gesture to accompany her statement.

Rally listened, closing her eyes, waiting for some pain. She wasn't able to figure out where they were headed.

The cushion dipped as the other woman joined her. "Sorry, I know this hurts. I'll be as quick and gentle as I can."

Rally wasn't holding out hope but being as she was used to only initial treatments, she would take what she could get. True to her word, this woman was quick and with a light touch. She even did her legs.

"Turn to your side then I can do your front."

Again, Rally listened.

"I'm Mino, by the way. Not really a doc but the best we've got under the circumstances." She lowered the shirt. "Let me put something else on the eye." She snapped off her gloves and tossed them in the small trash bag hanging on the wall before digging into the bag she'd brought with her. Uncapping the small jar, she then stuck in two fingers before smoothing it around Rally's eye.

The sting again was minor and she ignored it.

"There's a bathroom through there and — shit — I should have asked you first if you'd like a shower."

Shower? Lord, it sounded divine. It must have shown on her face.

"Okay, do you need help?"

She shook her head and rose to her feet. The shirt she wore fell to her knees. The bathroom had the similar colors. A clear-door shower beckoned to her. She moved closer, waiting for the moment this vision vanished and she woke back in that damn compound.

"Towels on the left. I'll leave some clean clothes and put more salve on you when you're done. Oh, and shampoo and conditioner are right inside there. I'll leave you alone now. Take your time."

The door closed and she was alone. She drew off the shirt and allowed it to flutter to the floor. A tear began the track down her face. She turned on the water and stepped in.

Hot water. The first on her skin since she'd been taken. Her tears mingled with the liquid streaming over her skin, washing away more than dirt.

When she had finished, having also done her hair, she turned off the water and stepped out, exhausted. She wrapped in a large fluffy towel and walked to the mirror.

There's what I look like. Thinner. Ugly bruises. She'd never been a beauty, or so she'd been told multiple times, but her name held worth. *Large circles below her eyes and the massive bruise around her left as well as the cut over it.* This was a stranger staring back at her. She stared for a while, taking the opportunity, and relearned her own face.

Knock. Knock.

"It's me, Mino. I heard the shower stop. Are you okay? I have clothes for you." The door opened and she entered. "Let me put the salve on again and I promise I'll leave you be." She moved behind her, placing clothes on the sink.

It didn't take long and Mino was heading for the door when she paused. "There's some food for you. We need to get some weight back on you." A kind smile and she was gone.

Rally picked up the clothes and almost cried again. They were clean, warm, and without holes. She pulled on the wool socks then drew on the thick sweatshirt and pink-gray warm-up pants.

Hair toweled off, she hung the towel up and padded to the door. The bed she'd used had been made to be like the other couch. Still, she longed to crawl back on it and sleep.

The floor beneath her shifted and she struggled not to fall. Her head spun as she attempted to shake off her exhaustion. Mino had said something about food. And that was necessary to remain ready for whatever was coming.

Even so, her hand wasn't all that steady when she depressed the black handle. Panic slammed her as she realized there was no way out for her. Short of trying to jump from an airplane. Nausea churned as she tried to control her fear.

She shook her head and dug deep for the cold mask she'd been taught to wear. The one where no emotions were shown, no expression allowed. These people were not her equals. She would *not* be cowed. All those years in captivity hadn't done it. These wouldn't either.

Three people placed their gazes on her as she stepped through the door. All expressions serious, and for a millisecond she debated locking herself in the room she'd just left. The redheaded female sat before a computer, sucking on a lollipop. Both men were imposing—not that the woman wasn't. Dark-haired, tan and capable were words that came to mind when she looked at the men.

31

One wore a suit and one had on jeans, cowboy boots, ball cap and a shirt that read *My Kinda Party*. They were the ones from the rainforest. As was the redhead.

Movement from the front had her spying Mino. She stepped in, gazed about and frowned. "God, y'all are scaring her." She beckoned. "Come on. I have a plate for you."

The redhead watched her cautiously as she walked by. The distrust lingering behind the deadpan stare didn't help set Rally at ease. She didn't respond, didn't offer up a smile of thanks, nor did she look away from the challenging stare.

Where is he?

She sat in the leather seat Mino indicated and took the offered plate before setting it on the small table. After removing the cover, she found scrambled eggs, toast, fruit and hash browns. Silverware and a glass were placed down.

"Wasn't sure what you wanted to drink but here's the juice. Unless you'd like coffee or something else?"

Tea would be heavenly. Lemon and peppermint.

"I think we need to find out who she is."

She stared at the knife, aware it would be a fool's errand.

"Don't even think about it." The redhead's tone vibrated with danger.

"We need fingerprints."

Nauseating fear hit her, overriding everything else, and she jerked from the seat, the food no longer tempting. She backed toward the cockpit only to stop when she hit a hard chest. Hands gripped her upper arms.

Christ, how many of them are there?

Panic overflowing, she twisted to see a tall, gaunt man behind her. Dark slashing eyebrows hid his eyes. He had presence and as she tried to back away he tightened his grip.

"Easy there."

She froze, eyes narrowing and moving over him again. Ethan? His voice was familiar even if she didn't recognize him. The shaggy hair was gone as well as the beard. His skin was pale but she had no doubt he would bulk up and tan soon.

"It's me. You remember me, right?"

She gazed at his hands touching her sweatshirt — the borrowed one — and her arms, then back to his face. His stare was steady.

"A nod would be great. Unless you'd like to talk?" Rally began to glance behind her but he captured her chin. "Eyes on me. They don't matter."

Some grumbled mutterings came up toward them. She nodded.

"Good. Now we'll sit, eat and talk." He released her and gestured to the chair she'd vacated.

He took the chair facing her and she rested her hands in her lap.

"You know —"

"Leave us, Mino."

"Fuck you, Ethan. I need to keep you alive."

"Mino." His warning was growled.

"Stuff it. I didn't fly all this way to have you sicker. Hold still while I put in another IV." She then left them as alone as they could be.

Rally waited. He leaned forward and picked up her fork, going for the hash browns. He ate a bite then put the utensil back on the plate.

"Now you." Her hesitation had him gesturing.

She reached out and grabbed a piece of toast. A small bite and she chewed slowly despite her clamoring for food.

"I need a name to call you," he said. "*You* isn't going to work." He took another bite.

The toast was uncomfortable to swallow. She had no wish to divulge who she was. *Used to be.*

"I'm assuming you can talk and you speak English as well as German." He leaned forward and ate some eggs. "Sweetheart, you can tell me or they will print you and run facial rec."

She went to put the toast back, her appetite fading, but his cocked brow stopped her. She tore off another small piece and nibbled it.

"If you don't want to talk, how about you write it down for me?" He waved to someone behind her.

A pad of paper and pen settled next to her. She lowered her gaze and focused on the piece of toast in her hand instead.

"I know you want to help her, Ethan. But this is getting old."

"Let it go, Anabelle Lee. She was there when I arrived. I haven't any clue how long she's been there. This is more than a bit overwhelming for her, I'm sure."

"So now we coddle?"

Ethan held her gaze and said in German, "You do know I won't hurt you, right?"

Do I know that? No. Hope, yes.

He ate another forkful of eggs then got more on the fork and held them to her mouth. "Open." When she didn't respond, he repeated his order in German and she found herself listening before she could stop it. She'd had too much time being conditioned to respond in an instant.

The eggs were warm and fluffy. She chewed them then swallowed, wishing she'd not been stubborn about eating and had enjoyed them when she'd had the chance. The look in his eyes told her he understood her thought. Holding out the fork to her, handle first, he offered it. She took it and began to eat.

Chapter Three

Ethan stood toward the back of the plane with his family. Valentino was in the cockpit with his brother who was flying them back home. His silent woman ate, shoveling in food as if she believed it would be taken from her. The manners were severely lacking and he knew if they were at Grams', she would have reprimanded her, but he let it go, aware she needed the sustenance.

"Why don't you let me print her?" Anabelle Lee's question was sharp.

He looked at his sister. "I don't think it's that simple."

"Why not?" Beau questioned. "We need to know who she is. She should be with her family." He readjusted his ball cap and gave a nod to the woman who'd finished eating and walked back to the small private room.

Ethan crossed his arms, his eyes often going back to the closed door to the aft stateroom. He'd been behind it with her at the start while they'd been delayed for takeoff by weather.

He glanced to his sister. She arched a brow back. "I've said it from the beginning."

"We get you're feeling a bit protective, Ethan." Mino joined them, exhaustion on her features.

This wasn't her thing. She was Masters' secretary. She didn't earn her paycheck as they did, humping it out in the bush. No wonder she looked beat. Not one word of complaint passed her lips, though.

"But?"

"Whoever she is, she's hiding something. Most rescued hostages would be screaming their name to anyone who would listen, desperate to get home. This one, nothing. Not verbal or written. It's like she's fine not being home."

"I'm sure she's scared. I did after all threaten to kill her as well. For all she knows she's gone from the frying pan into the fire."

They all exchanged looks and he sat back down, his strength still lacking. "Run it." He closed his eyes only to crack them open at a touch on his arm. He hated how he wanted to flinch from it all.

"I'll get them." Anabelle Lee made the statement then walked away.

"Grams will want to see you." Beau sat across from him.

"How is she?"

"Missing you. Refusing to give up hope." Beau's phone rang and he answered after a brief screen check. "We're bringing him home, Masters. Malnourished, ornery, but alive." He grunted. "Mino, Masters wants to talk to you."

She neared and took the phone. "Yes, sir?" As she headed away, he put his gaze back on his cousin.

"You need more sleep." As usual, Beau was straightforward. "You look like shit. It's been one hell of a year. Can I get you anything?"

"A woman?" he joked.

Beau's smile didn't reach his eyes. In fact, that gaze swirled with anger. Imposing and deadly. "If I thought you meant it, I would have Giovanni land this plane and get you as many as you want to believe you could handle."

Ethan scratched his neck. Outside, the sun ducked behind some dark clouds. He yawned and Beau jerked his head toward the door. With another yawn, he rose and entered the small room as Anabelle left, sporting a serious scowl. Ethan stepped into the room and found his silent woman on the couch. She sat on the far end, head down, and doing her best to become invisible.

"We both know you know I'm here. Look at me."

She obeyed. Her gaunt features bothered him. Beneath all the dirt she'd been covered in, and in the large clothing she wore, he couldn't see much, but she looked younger than he'd believed her to be with his second assumption. He sat on the sofa across from her then stretched out.

"My sister, Anabelle Lee, will have your name in no time so you may as well tell me." He angled his head to stare at her.

Her eyes were wide in her face as she shook her head. She moved her lips and for a moment he wondered if she would speak. No such luck.

"Rest. We're not going anywhere up here."

Rain began to hit the windows and he readjusted before rising and grabbing blankets, handing one set to her, then he lay back down. After ten minutes of silence, he returned his attention to her. She was curled on her side, engulfed by the bedding.

His heart lurched then he closed his eyes as well. He had to rest and heal. He had a score to settle. There would be retribution.

A tap on his foot had him nearly jumping out of his skin from the expectation of a kick to his ribs. He opened his eyes and found Beau standing there, larger than life. Once it registered he wasn't a prisoner any longer, he breathed easier. He looked to his left, almost shocked she wasn't awake, then he recalled how stealthy Beau was.

Gesturing to take leave, he sat up. Outside the rain continued pelting the windows. His body protested his movements, desperate for more decent rest, but he got to his feet and at the last moment draped his comforter over her.

Ethan caught himself before stroking her hair. He turned and moved by Beau, whose raised eyebrow informed him he'd seen the behavior. They stepped into the rest of the plane.

Valentino was back in the galley and gave him a nod as he headed back into the cockpit with two coffees.

"What'd you find?" He lowered to a chair and put up with Mino hooking him to another nutrient-packed IV. *How'd she get so many here?* Seconds after the question flashed in his mind he recalled the jet was fully stocked.

"This Rolf," Anabelle said, sitting with an alcoholic drink in hand, "is gone. I put in your sketch and we're running but nothing is popping. Fucker's a ghost."

He eyed her drink. A cold beer would be wonderful. Or whatever his sister had in her glass. *Hopefully it's not from Masters' private stash.* Then again, knowing Anabelle Lee it was.

"Anything about what that compound was? Drugs?"

"You didn't see anything when you ran?"

He thought back to his first escape. "Not other than a lot of people I killed." His chest hurt as he thought of his cell. Small. Confined. Rat infested. Sweat beaded on his brow and he fought the urge to pace. He wouldn't let it beat him.

I'm stronger than this.

He breathed deeply through his nose. "The area's been marked, right?"

"Fuck yeah. Masters has been read in. He's sent a team." Beau got up for some cranberry juice.

Ethan knew it. Until they were home the man was off alcohol. Beau didn't drink on missions. Ethan's unease didn't lessen so he sat up to go over what they'd discovered.

"Drugs makes sense given the location but I don't recall seeing any as I ran. Maybe she knows."

Anabelle finished her drink and rose for another. He watched her then stared at his cousin. "She's lost weight."

"You being kidnapped was hard on her. All of us. But hell, she's your sister."

Mino walked over and joined them. "How did you find him?"

"I had some contacts who came through." Beau shrugged without shame and Mino leaned back, understanding in her gaze. Anabelle returned and reclined in her seat.

"So," he said, trying to break the tension. "What have I missed?"

As he'd hoped, the stress on their faces melted away as they laughed. A *ping* had Anabelle sitting forward. She typed on her Surface before whistling low.

"What?" He stared at the IV bag, wishing it weren't attached to him.

The screen was shoved in his line of sight.

"I had a hit on your mystery woman."

Instantly intrigued, he sat forward. Anabelle unsnapped the screen from the keyboard. Beauregard reached for his as well and pulled up the information with a low whistle.

Ethan read and wasn't sure what he saw was real. He went over it a few times then lay it on his lap. His mind whirled with all of the potential scenarios.

"Get this out of my hand before I rip it out."

Mino did, swiftly removing the IV stuck in his skin, and made note she hadn't asked what was on the file. The moment he was free, he rose and beelined it.

"Let me handle this," he said, and slipped behind the door.

His prisoner — or rescuer — lay in the same position, burrowed beneath all the blankets. Unwilling to wake her, he sat on his sleeping spot and stretched out his legs, then began flipping through the file yet again.

He dozed but woke when she stirred. He cracked open his eyes to observe her as she emerged from her cocoon. Her gaze snapped to him then to the bathroom door. Ethan held still as she decided whether or not to go. After a bit, she moved warily to the door and slipped inside. He yawned and waited. When the door opened again, he remained immobile until she returned to her side of the bed. Then he lifted his lids and stared at her.

"Hello, princess."

* * * *

He puffed on the thick cigar and stared up at the cerulean sky. Beneath his bare feet, the white sand was warm and he scrunched his toes in it.

"Boss."

Turning his head, he stared at the man hastening up to him, the focus on him and not the women walking around in nothing more than string bikini bottoms, the sun having turned them into golden goddesses.

"Yes?"

He took the paper offered and read it. A heavy exhalation and he grasped his stogie, removing it from his mouth. "I assume this has been verified."

"Twice, sir."

Damn, I liked that place in Venezuela. "Fine. Eliminate it."

"And the people?"

"Kill everyone. I want nothing remaining. And when he lands, bring him to me." He put the cigar back in and pushed his hands into the pockets of his shorts.

"Yes, sir. He's due in three hours."

"Good. I'd like to know what happened. That will be all." He headed toward the turquoise water and stopped when his toes hit the liquid. *A minor setback. So what if it was a multi-million-dollar venture. It won't take long to set up another.*

After ten minutes in the sun, he turned and strolled back up the beach to the small hut where he stepped into a hidden elevator and went down. When it opened, he walked out into a huge room with maps all over and more technology than people would even imagine could be in one place.

Time to get back to work.

* * * *

Rally stared at him, desire to bolt splashed all over her face, the most expression he'd seen on her yet. He tossed the electronic device to the cushion by his left thigh. "Still pretending you don't speak? I happen to know you speak several languages. German wasn't listed." He lifted his brows. "Say something."

She swallowed as her face returned to the blank slate.

"How about I tell you what I know so far?"

She clutched the blanket at her side but that was the sole outward sign of her discomfort.

"You were lost three years ago when a flight you were on disappeared over the Coral Sea."

The corner of her mouth twitched but she maintained her silence.

"You're the youngest in your family. A princess. Three older sisters and two brothers. Youngest but definitely the most outspoken." He leaned forward, resting arms on top of his thighs. "Or were."

Seriously, a fucking princess? Why didn't I know about this?

"Aren't you excited to be going home?"

She gazed at her hands and he felt that damn wrenching in his heart. A woman who'd been prisoner who was less than excited to return home where she was a princess.

"I'm going to put a call in to the king and let him know his daughter — long-lost and presumed dead — Zahra Kidjo is coming home.

"No."

His eyebrows shot up to his hairline. Her voice was husky with lack of use yet it still hit him squarely. She'd spoken.

Rally willed her heart to slow down. If they weren't flying miles above the earth, she would have made a run for it. Zahra — a name she'd not been called in years — echoed through her mind. All those memories — she'd begun to wonder if they hadn't been made up — must be true.

Am I even that person anymore? Doubtful.

"No?"

She dampened her lips and dug for the cold arrogance and royal swagger she used to own in spades. It didn't work as it once had. That level of cockiness had been long since beaten out of her.

She swallowed and tried again. "No."

"Am I hearing you right and you're telling me you have no wish to go back to your life?"

"I would rather not be tossed in the media storm that would come with returning." The words felt foreign coming off her lips, it had been so long since she'd spoken. Did they still make sense as they did in her mind?

He weighed her statement and she wound her hands in the blankets, wishing she'd not lost her courage.

"What happened?"

Bile rose and she gulped it back. "I only recall parts. There wasn't any reason for me to rehash it."

He sat forward and took her hand after digging it free from the covers. Her pulse skittered at the simple gesture.

"Take your time."

This man was an enigma to her. He'd threatened her life, protected her, killed men after going through what he'd endured, and now sat here calming and trying to reassure her.

"We were flying from New Zealand to—" She struggled to recall. "Somewhere. I'm sorry, I can't seem to remember. I'd given a talk at a dinner." Multiple images flashed and she shook her head trying to sort them all out. "Clear day then a flicker—" She pursed her lips and squeezed her eyes shut only to open them seconds later. "Maybe a pulse is a better word. It went over the plane and we dropped."

Her heart constricted as she relived the numbing fear which had assaulted her. Her stomach in her throat as they dropped from the sky, then something she couldn't grasp, before waking in a cell.

"I don't remember the crash, just waking up in a small cell. I, of course, was loud and belligerent, as I always had been. That's when the beatings began. At some point they moved me to Venezuela but I'm not sure where I'd been previously." Her temples throbbed.

He moved his thumb over the back of her hand. The motion was soothing and intimate. "After all this time, why not the excitement to return home?"

How can I word this so it makes sense to him? She stared out of the window at the rain sluicing down the pane. "You were there for a year." She ignored her dry throat. "Are you wanting to be tossed in front of cameras of the viperous paparazzi unrelenting in their pursuit to find out all you endured? Every minute detail? Forcing you to relive it over and over? On top of that I would be forced to attend functions and be a proper princess. I've been a prisoner for years, three according to you."

He didn't so much as blink. "You're hiding something." He tightened his hold when she attempted to draw her hand away. "I need to know."

She turned her head to look at him, throat tired from talking. He didn't deflect his gaze, nor did she. Static charged the air between them. They'd both endured hell, an act which bonded them together in ways others would never be able to understand. He'd saved her on a level he may never know.

Just tell him. It wasn't complete in her mind and she despised not having all the facts.

"I will make them pay." He moved some of her hair away from where it fell forward before tucking it behind her ear. She locked onto his stare as his rough hand touched her skin. Gentle. His fingertips traced the edge of her cut and bruise. "I swear."

She believed him. Whether for him, or was this so important, she couldn't say.

"Zahra."

She shook her head slightly. "Rally."

A small smile kicked up his lips. "Of course it is."

The clearing throat almost had her lunging out of her skin. Ethan didn't move. Not for another tick of time. When he retreated, she was torn between relief and frustration for reasons she wasn't about to contemplate.

When he deprived her of his touch, she snuck a peek to see who stood there. The imposing man. Well, they all were but he was much larger than the others.

"We land in less than sixty," he said, his drawl thick as he watched her with green eyes. "What are we doing with her?"

She barely breathed as she awaited her fate. Ethan squeezed her hand. "She's coming home with me."

"She's what?" This from the redhead.

"I didn't stutter. She's got some memories locked away, and if she's at her palace in Africa we won't have access to her." He released her hand and stood. "She stays with me until Rolf is dead."

So he wanted her there for his own revenge reasons, not because he cared about her. She ignored the sting that created in her gut. She reprimanded herself for ever having a slight hope. She was a commodity, always had been. Always would be.

For her, things zipped by in a blur after that statement. They came in to land and rain still fell. Correction, it was more a snow or sleet mixture. Dread filled her as the unknown loomed before her. She peered out of the window and saw a single vehicle waiting — a white SUV, wipers moving and exhaust fumes coming from the tailpipe.

"Let's go."

Rally looked up to find Anabelle Lee standing there. The woman's expression was less than hospitable ergo she didn't tarry in rising. There was no press waiting as she stepped into the rain.

The cold took her breath. How long had it been since she'd been anything other than sweaty? She tucked her hands inside the long sleeves of her loaned sweatshirt. While the bite from the cold wetness bordered on painful, she relished it. It meant she wasn't where she had been.

She walked down the steps between Mino and Anabelle Lee. Part of her longed to twist around and look for Ethan. She stumbled and was held upright by the redhead beside her.

"You hurt my brother and I swear you'll wish to be back in Venezuela." The southern drawl was anything but welcoming.

Rally didn't respond. She had no desire to hurt Ethan. *I wonder where I am.* This airport was small. Around the size of some of the executive ones she'd flown into in the past.

"Get in."

Ethan's order had her opening the door and climbing into the back. No one was there but it was warm and dry. Seconds later, Mino slipped in as well. She gave Rally a smile. The back opened and some gear was tossed in. Through the window, she watched as two more people came down the steps. She recognized one but the other she didn't.

The familial resemblance couldn't be missed. Good-looking men but her heart didn't react until she saw the man she owed her life to. There was something about him, even being malnourished and thinner than the others.

"You need a blanket?"

"No, thank you."

Mino smiled. "You do talk. I'd heard rumors." She sobered. "Things will be okay, I know it. These guys are the best."

Rally returned her attention outside. The sleet had picked up and someone had slung a coat over Ethan's narrow shoulders. The five stood there talking for a bit before another round of hugs was exchanged and the one she didn't know left with his brother — she supposed — and headed for a vehicle she'd not noticed until now. Ethan and the other two approached.

Beau got behind the wheel, Anabelle Lee got in the passenger seat and Ethan climbed in the back, sliding onto the seat next to her.

She dozed in the car, unable to stay awake. She woke later to find she was using Ethan as a pillow. His arm was around her and someone had covered her with a blanket. They'd slowed and she sat up with a yawn and peered out of the window.

They drove up a drive lined with trees. The man beside her trembled and she reached out and gave his hand a slight squeeze.

The house was a large two-story with a surrounding porch on both levels. It was painted white with some nice stone facing on the parts she could see. They came to a stop before the stairs that led up to the second level.

"You sure you don't need us to come in?"

Ethan opened the door. "We'll be fine. I think right now we could use some solid sleep."

"I'll be by later with some food and to check on you." Beau looked in the rearview mirror as he spoke.

"I know. Thanks."

Mino gripped her hand. "You'll be fine. I'll be by to check on you as well."

"Thank you."

"Come on, Rally." Ethan stepped out and held his hand toward her.

She took it and together they walked up one half of the split stairs to the front door. The cold icy daggers pelted her and she shivered as he typed in a code.

She followed him inside, and when the door clicked behind them, she realized she was now alone with the man in a foreign country.

He turned and looked at her, the emotion in his gaze unreadable for her. After clearing his throat, he said, "The house will be warm in a minute. The kitchen and everything is up on this level and the bedrooms are downstairs. I'll show you to yours."

Chapter Four

Ethan stood in his shower, the mist so thick he wouldn't be able to see out of the glass even if he were inclined to look. He braced his hands along the smooth tile of the walls and cried. A mixture of relief and anger poured from him. He clenched his hands into fists and tipped his head up to take a direct spray.

When he didn't have any energy left to remain, he turned off the water, killing the multi-directional sprays. He opened the door and stepped onto the fluffy rug, scrunching his toes as he reached for a towel. Drying his face, he strode to the mirror then wiped away the steam to stare at his reflection. His razor waited there along the twin sinks and he thought about it but was too shaky to shave.

Not even close to the man he'd once been. Gazing away, he stared at the scars left behind from the rats and those from the torture. He finished drying off and hung up the towel before padding naked into the rest of his master suite. He'd not been sure he would ever see this place again.

A fire blazed in the hearth warming his naked body. He stared at the king-size platform bed calling his name. Pivoting on his heels, he went back to his walk-in closet before he recalled the drawers on his bed frame. He went there where he grabbed a pair of sweats. They pretty much fell off his thin frame and he tied them before heading to bed. He drew back the thick comforter and climbed in.

Beau said that they'd put clean sheets on his bed. Personally, he didn't care. He was getting a real bed with sheets. One final look to the security panel to assure himself all was safe, and he closed his eyes.

* * * *

He woke when the *beep* came, jolting from dead sleep to wide awake. It took him a moment to register where he was. He peered out of one of the large windows and was surprised to see snow falling. They didn't get a lot of that in Georgia. He rose and reached for a zipper hoodie and drew it on.

On his way up to the main part of his house, he stopped to look in on Rally. She was buried beneath the mound of blankets on the queen bed. Closing the door quietly, he walked to his stairs and headed up.

He came in at the kitchen area where Beau and Anabelle were fixing some food. "You know we can't hold Grams off much longer. You need to go see her." Beau sucked his thumb clean and poured the batter on the skillet.

"Mino sent some clothing for the princess," Anabelle said.

There wasn't any way to avoid the dislike in his sister's tone. "I'll go see Grams tomorrow." He scratched the back of his neck. "What are you two doing here?"

"It's been two weeks since we dropped you off." His sister opened the orange juice and poured him a glass.

He blinked. "Two weeks? Fuck, I don't even remember getting up to take a piss."

"How's your princess doing?"

"You say that with such disdain, sis. She's sleeping."

"I don't trust her."

He arched an eyebrow. "I do. She saved my life. That's all I need to know."

Anabelle kept her mouth shut for all of three seconds. "I realize you feel some sort of debt to her for that. I owe her for saving you but there's something else going on with her."

Ethan nodded. "I don't disagree." He sliced his gaze to his cousin. "You ever get tired of Theta Corps and you'd make a damn good housekeeper. Although maybe the French maid outfit wouldn't work the best for you."

"Stop acting like you can't cook. Grams made sure all of us could. And I'll have you know I'd look absolutely adorable in an apron. A cute one with ruffles that accentuates my ass." Beau smirked at him.

"You don't even let the woman you're with know you can cook, do you?"

"Fuck no. My part in the relationship is making sure she's pleasured in bed. Her part, cooking."

"God, you're fucking antiquated," Anabelle Lee snapped.

"Stop, please." He held up his hands, desperate to ward off the impending argument although, after what he'd been through, it was music to his ears. "Let me fill you in on what she told me on the plane."

He had to redirect this conversation or it would only get more out of hand. Beau was a player. Made no bones about it. But he loved tweaking his cousin's nose about what a woman should or shouldn't do. He knew it was all bluster because Grams would take a switch to him for acting as if he actually believed that.

They ate and Ethan took his pills as he let them in on why he wanted to have her here with him. Ethan's appetite wasn't huge but he made an effort.

"Any news on Rolf and where he may have gone?"

Beau helped himself to a drink and shook his head. "No. Masters said—"

The doorbell rang. His body tensed and he reached beneath the counter for the SIG he kept there.

"I'll get it," Anabelle said. She left only to return moments later with Masters himself in tow.

Snow dotted the man's shoulders and black leather newsboy cap. "Damn good to see you, Ethan."

"To be seen as well. Care for some food? My resident bitch made it up for me."

"Suck this," Beau said, grabbing himself with an eye roll.

The man nodded before he fixed himself a plate and sat beside him at the bar. His dark skin gleamed beneath the lights as he shrugged out of his coat and took off his hat. Black? Native? Perhaps a combination of both. Ethan hadn't been able to determine it yet. His boss was more secretive than the lot of them.

"So what can I do for you?" he asked his boss.

"Wanted to give you an update and had to see you for myself." Masters dug in with relish to the breakfast. "The team I sent in found nothing."

"What?" he thundered.

"Rephrase. They found nothing useful. A cleaner team had gone in before we got men back there. Everyone was slaughtered and left there. Probably as a sign. Either way, there's nothing for us to go on."

"Except the princess," Anabelle said, reaching for another slice of bacon.

"Right, your princess. Where is she?"

Protectiveness raced over him, especially with the way he said princess. "Sleeping — and no, I'm not waking her."

Masters raised an eyebrow but didn't stop eating. "I'm not a patient man. I'm going to wish to speak to her. And soon."

Ethan drank his juice. "She's resting."

Beau crossed massive arms. He'd always been the larger of the two boys but now Ethan felt damn near puny next to him. "We'll make her available when she's ready and not a minute before."

Anabelle Lee stood next to Beau and added her scowl to the mix. He was relieved they had his back even though he was well aware of their skepticism toward her.

"He's our family and she's under our protection now." Anabelle Lee made it clear she didn't like Masters challenging them.

Their boss scowled. "We need to learn what she knows."

"She doesn't remember it all." Ethan rose and got some more juice, sharing a look of thanks with his sister. "Why don't you spill what you know."

"What are you talking about?" Masters refuted.

"We all have known you long enough to pick up on when you have something. So just spill." He poured it then put the rest back in the fridge.

"I need a secure computer."

Ethan shrugged and waved them on after him. They made their way down the hall past the descending stairs to the bedrooms, on to his den. Once inside, he headed to the table positioned to the right of the fireplace, placed his juice on the edge and pressed a button on the underside of the lip. The top morphed from the dark hue of the wood to a clear screen.

"Here you go. There are USBs along the side, or you can just set it down, it'll pull the information from it." A large screen slid over the stonework on the hearth's wall. He gazed to the windows and stared out at the falling snow. He wanted to just go for a walk in it and indulge in the silence. Maybe Rally would like to join him. "If you need the room secure, we can do that as well. They can't see in from outside to this room, if you're wondering."

Masters pulled a small device from his pocket and plugged it in. A wealth of files popped up on the flat screen. "The system is secure?"

"Yes." He hesitated for a moment then went to one of the leather chairs and sank into the softness.

"Never realized how much of a fucking geek you truly are," Anabelle said as she brought him his juice and set it beside him on the small table.

Ethan winked at her. Masters opened a file and sent it to the large screen on the wall. "Theta has been delving into the disappearances with these planes. These crashes." He put air quotes around the last word.

"Why the suspicion?" Beau braced his hands on the table as he stared at the images of all the planes.

"We check everything that happens around the world. Entire planes vanishing without a trace may not be important to most of the world because they're not from one of the superpower countries, but it is to us. And suspicious. It happens only to countries most people don't give a damn exists." He tapped another picture and sent it up to the large screen as well.

Ethan sat up a bit, noting he wasn't alone in whose attention had been snagged.

"All we get—weeks later—are bodies and parts. Chunks of metal, fuselages, and the like. Never a black box stating its flight path. Never a survivor."

Narrowing his eyes, Ethan flexed his fingers around the blue-tinted glass. "Until now, you mean."

He didn't appreciate the look on Masters' face.

* * * *

Rally stared out at the snow falling. Fat, thick flakes dropped from the sky in a steady pattern. She sat curled up in the chair in the room he'd put her in. Unsure of how much time had gone by since they'd arrived, she couldn't even begin to fathom how much she'd been sleeping. Her body still cried out for more but she was sore and had to get up and move around.

Her marks had healed more and the bruise on her face had faded. The cut lingered as did remnants of the discoloration but it wasn't as it had been. She wanted to leave the room but wasn't sure if it was allowed, so had opted instead to do a few laps around in it then take the chair.

The large chair swallowed her and the fluffy blanket around her kept her even warmer than she'd expected. She looked at one hand, noting the scars, broken nails and overall beat-up condition of them. The days of never looking out of place had gone far, far away.

Tucking her hand back in, she rested her head on the back of the chair, allowing the silence of her world to sink in. Her stomach growled but she ignored it. She'd been hungry before and she would survive being that way once more.

"Oh, you're awake."

The masculine voice jolted her and she jumped up, eyes downcast, doing her best not to tremble. What would the punishment be this time?

"Rally?" Soft footsteps moved toward her. "Come on, princess, look at me. It's me, Ethan."

She waited in silence as his touch brought her head up. His eyes were sympathetic as he gazed down at her.

"You're safe now, Rally. No one will hurt you again. Okay?"

It didn't sink in for a few moments but he never moved, just continued to watch her until she nodded.

He gave her a ghost of a smile as his thumb brushed the underside of her bottom lip. "You and I are fucked up, Rally, but we'll get through it. I didn't mean to disturb you, I just came to check on you. You've been out for two weeks. We both have."

Really? It'd been that long? Real sleep in a real bed without worrying about creatures or anything else attacking her.

"I thought you may be hungry or would like to go outside and take a walk with me?"

She took in his jeans that hung on his frame, and the thick long-sleeved shirt. He had on hiking boots. She gazed down and saw her socked feet, sweatpants and a sweatshirt.

"Don't worry about clothes, princess. Mino sent some things over. She bought it all new so it's not anything someone else had. The bags are over there by the dresser. Shower, whatever you want, and I'll meet you upstairs in the living room."

She'd seen the bags but hadn't touched them, not realizing they were for her. She gave him a small nod.

"Good." He stepped back and went to the door where he paused. "One more thing. I hope that sleep didn't make you forget how to talk."

She shook her head and he grinned before slipping out. Her heart skipped a few beats at the way his blue eyes had sparkled when he'd smiled.

Fifteen minutes later, she trekked up the stairs to the kitchen. The house was beautiful and she moved slowly, taking in the gleaming dark-brown railing and the off-white walls.

He was at the sink when she hit the top. Ethan turned his head and gazed over his shoulder at her, taking in her attire. "Ready to eat something?"

She nodded and walked closer to him, hands retreating into the sleeves of the long shirt she'd picked to wear. Mino had gotten her a bra, new underwear, and almost anything she could have wanted. It had been so long since she'd worn any underclothes, it had been weird putting them on.

"Do you want a hearty meal or something lighter?"

She lifted her shoulders, willing to accept whatever he allowed her to eat. He rinsed his hands then dried them on a paper towel before throwing it away. "I'm not going to ask you yes or no questions, Rally. I want you to talk to me."

She swallowed a few times and wet her lips. "Anything is fine."

He moved by her to the fridge and poured her some juice. "Drink this to start. We'll take a walk then maybe you'll be more confident in what you want."

His fingers glanced along hers as he passed over the glass. Her gut tightened and a feeling she'd not had in a long time moved along her skin. Want. She dropped her gaze, unwilling to risk him seeing it in her eyes. "Thank you," she said before sipping the drink.

"Hmm, that didn't seem too hard for you to say. Perhaps we're making progress." He returned to the counter and continued cleaning. "Sit down on the stool."

She followed his order and forced herself to continue drinking even though she didn't like orange juice. She wasn't about to refuse it.

"Stop," he said.

She paused with it partway to her mouth for another sip. Doing her best to hide the shaking in her hand, she put the glass back to the marbled countertop. His eyebrows were slashed again and he scowled.

"Why didn't you say you don't like orange juice?" He held up his hand. "Never mind, I know." He plucked it from her hand and gave her another glass, empty this time. "Go to the fridge and get what you want. Or do you want coffee? We're going to have to work together on this, princess. You won't ever get yelled at for not wanting something here. And if there's something specific you want, ask for it. You're not a prisoner any longer."

She slid from the stool and made her way to the fridge where she pressed the glass under the water option on the door.

"Lord," he muttered from behind her. "Let's take a walk."

She finished the water, thirst quenched enough for the moment. He handed her a large coat that swallowed her. A grin tugged at the corners of his mouth. "Well, you'll be warm." After which he put a hat with earflaps on her head. "Mino said she'd kill me if I let you get sick. And that woman has a mean streak in her a mile wide. Don't let her innocent look fool you. Not for a second. I'm scared of her." He winked.

They walked to the door. He grabbed a coat as well and together they left the house. She inhaled sharply with the slap of the frigid air. They were protected from the snow under the roof but the steps had snow on them.

"Get a lot of snow at your home?"

She shook her head and took a step forward before stopping. The hand at her back prevented her from retreating behind him.

"You want to go, go. You're safe here. The property is fenced, a security system in place. I've coded you into the house so you can get in and out whenever you want. Also to the gate at the end of the property."

He put her arm in the crook of his and together they went down to the landing then turned left and walked that way to the ground.

"We've not had this much snow for a long time. I can't recall when it was last up past my ankles." He dipped his head and whispered, warm breath brushing along her ear. "Conversation works much better when both parties are talking."

She didn't pick up on any malice in his tone, just lighthearted teasing. "I like listening to your voice. It's soothing." She clamped her mouth shut. *I can't believe I just said that.*

"Always good to know." His words were still right by her ear, warming it despite it being covered by the earflap. "I'd be able to return the sentiment if you spoke more." They walked to the woods and strolled through the snow-covered trees as more snow fell around them. "Do you realize I've never heard you say my name and, let's face it, we've already kissed."

"That was me getting water to you."

"She does speak," he teased.

She smiled. He placed a hand along the side of her face, thumb stroking below her eye. "You do have a point, though. It wasn't a real kiss."

Her breathing hitched and her nipples tightened. Would he kiss her? He leaned closer, ever so slowly, and paused right before his mouth touched hers.

"When you're ready for it, say my name, princess. And I'll rectify that kiss situation." He backed off and began walking again.

Her knees trembled. She wanted his kiss. Almost shouting his name, she refused to let it by her lips. Instead she struck out after him, taking the initiative to slip her arm back through his. Watching him from the corner of her eye, she noticed the kick up of his lips when she did.

"You should expect to see Beau or Anabelle Lee around here at any given time. Their properties touch mine and they are nosy."

"You were gone for a long time. Why wouldn't they want to check on you?" She tipped her head back and let the snow land on her face, the bite refreshing. "Plus, they don't trust me."

"They will."

She let that go and enjoyed the walk. It wasn't a long one, yet she was still ready to lie down when she returned. *I don't know how I did what I did there if this is so taxing to my body.*

He checked his phone and sighed. "Just a heads-up, princess. There's a visitor at the house."

His words had her wanting to curl into a ball. "You would expect people to be by to see you."

"You'd think," he muttered. "However, this is different."

The house came into view and she stared at the smoke rising from the dual chimneys. "How?"

They headed up the steps to the door. Inside she could see a woman moving around by the breakfast bar.

"Because this is my grandmother." He encouraged her in, followed, and closed the door behind them. "Hello, Grams."

The woman stopped everything, dusted off her hands, and placed one over her mouth. Tears shone in her eyes as she hurried toward them. Rally stepped away from him as Grams opened her arms to hug him.

"My Ethan. I knew you would come home. I *knew* it."

Rally averted her gaze, not wanting to intrude on their reunion. Slowly she inched by and retreated back outside. Standing at the barrier of the porch, she gazed about his property. Snow covered everything, holding down the noise and creating a world of silence. She curved her hands on the rail.

He wanted her here where she would be accessible. She wasn't a fool but this was a private time. He'd said she could go out on her own but her energy wasn't all that much and she was cold. Still, she trekked down the stairs and slipped back off into the woods.

She found a tree trunk that had been cut and brushed the snow off it before sitting on it. Pulling her legs up to her chest, she wrapped her arms around them and rested her chin on her knees. Snow continued to fall but she ignored it and wondered about her future.

Maybe I should have let him send me home. Being home didn't send feelings of warmth through her. More akin to dread.

The wind picked up and she shuddered.

"You know he's going to wonder where you went, darlin'."

One second he wasn't there, then the next, the man Ethan called Beauregard stepped into her line of sight.

She shook her head, disagreeing with that assessment.

"Oh, trust me, he will." He moved closer, his green eyes piercing. "I know you can talk, so this shaking your head, not gonna fly with me."

She scrunched her toes up in the boots, grateful they were warm. Her ass, however, was getting cold. "He's with his grandmother. I didn't think I was needed to witness their private time."

"You decided to come back out in the cold when you've been by the equator for the past few years?"

She shrugged. "It's so beautiful." Fear leeched into her. "He said I could be out here."

"Not here to disagree. I think you should have someone near in case you get too tired to go farther. You're still recouping. If you want to stay out here, fine. I'll be near. If you want to walk more, also fine, but I will be your shadow."

The finality in his tone told her it would have been pointless to argue with him even if she were inclined to do such a thing. Which she wasn't.

She dug deep and found a tiny sliver of courage and held his gaze. "Can you tell me about where I am?"

Chapter Five

He didn't stop the tears which flew down his face. His grams had been his sole parental figure growing up and he loved her more than anything.

"I never gave up on you, Ethan. *Never.* I knew you'd be home with us once again."

He drew back and wiped the tears from her eyes. "It's not safe, Grams. They know who I am."

"They don't know as much as they think they do," she said. "You survived and came home."

"I'm sorry I put you through this."

"It's your job. It's what you do. I worry about all three of you in your clandestine jobs. I worry when you walk down the street to get groceries. It's my job to worry." She stepped back. "You need fattening up."

It didn't shock him she knew he worked for some group. They'd never been able to keep anything from her.

"Grams, I want you to meet someone who was a prisoner there as well." He reached behind him. "Her name is—" There wasn't anyone there. He jerked around and she wasn't there.

Where'd she go?

"You find her and I'll make some food. You need to eat more." She shooed him away and walked to his kitchen.

Ethan retreated downstairs to her bedroom and knocked once before opening the door to find it empty. "Rally?" He checked the bathroom then headed up the stairs.

"I'll be back, Grams."

"I'll be here."

He shrugged into the jacket he'd removed and stepped outside.

"She's in the woods. Beau is watching over her."

He turned his head to find his sister leaning against the side of his house. "She's in the woods?"

"She left when you and Grams had your reunion. Beau volunteered to watch her and since I didn't want to, I let him go." She moved toward him, hair loose around her shoulders, brilliant against the rich black of her coat.

"What's your problem with her?"

"I don't trust her." Anabelle Lee stared at him with blue eyes like his own. "You said she wasn't held in a cell. Why didn't she leave? Why would she stay there and be in on what you suffered?"

"To be fair, that was the only time I saw her there. And let's face it, Anabelle Lee. She's not exactly forceful here. She barely speaks and keeps her gaze averted. That's not the sign of a woman who's plotting something. That's someone who's been beaten into submission." He kicked the rail. "She's scared of her own shadow. Why can't you see that? Did you miss the whip marks on her body or the bruise on her face along with the cut?"

"You can argue all you want, Ethan." She crossed her arms. "We're both aware some people will go to any length to get you to believe something and let your guard down."

He narrowed his gaze. "Speaking from experience with Carlo?"

Hers narrowed as well. "Don't go there."

"Why not him but a woman who's been through hell?"

"Because you've had something against any man around me since they first started looking in my direction. You and Beau both."

"As if you've not been a bitch to women in my life."

"Until she spills it all, I'm not trusting her."

Her response, while understandable, frustrated him. "I don't care, just be nice to her. It's not Lexy who's fine with the attitude. She's not like that."

"I don't coddle. And she's supposed to be a princess. She should be used to cold and uncaring."

"Don't be foolish. Not my care. I want you to be nice to her. Regardless of your feelings, she's —"

"*Supposed* to be a princess."

"Three years and eight months, Anabelle Lee. Christ, can't you cut her a little slack? She hasn't crumbled. I'd say that says a lot about her." He descended the steps and tracked Rally from the footprints in the snow, needing her with him for a reason he'd rather not explore further.

He heard her before he saw her. Ethan drew up and waited. Her voice was stronger and more assured than with him. He scowled, disliking that fact. Striding into view, he growled low in his throat at the realization that Rally wore Beau's jacket. It swallowed her. She sat on a stump, more animated than he'd ever seen her.

Not that it would take much to be more than how she's been.

Beau had her enthralled by whatever he told her. Then again, perhaps it was Rally who'd enthralled the man who loved women. All women.

"Rally."

She turned her head in his direction and he swore if she weren't seated she'd have hidden behind his cousin. He forced himself to remain calm and not snap.

I'm in trouble if she's doing this to me.

"Grams wants to meet you," he said, nodding at his cousin, unsure he could say anything without sounding like a possessive ass to him. "She's fixing some food for us to eat." He held out his hand, beckoning to her.

She slid off the stump and began approaching him before stopping and shrugging out of Beau's jacket. "Thank you," she said softly.

"Anytime, darlin'." He put it back on.

He glared at his cousin and waited for her to take his hand. She moved slowly but soon enough her hand was in his and he curled his fingers around hers, grateful — mostly — she wasn't cold.

"You didn't have to come outside," he said as they headed back to the house.

"I wanted to be outside. You said it was okay if I went."

He squeezed her fingers. "It was fine."

Beau fell into step on the other side of her and he wanted to punch his cousin and get him away from her. Staring at him over the top of her head, he cocked an eyebrow. Beau grinned and gave him a look that set his teeth on edge. Flirting was as natural as breathing to Beau and Ethan didn't want it around Rally.

"Is there anything else you need? I know Mino sent a bag of things for you but Beau will be making a trip into town for us. Do you need anything else picked up?"

"No thank you."

Her voice was low and subdued once more and it grated on his nerves. Meeting Beau's gaze, he didn't know what to make of his cousin's confusion as well. They didn't rush and he continually rubbed his thumb along the back of her hand while they progressed.

"You'll be fine. She'll love you."

At the door, he stopped and waited for her to nod in understanding. Then they went inside. The scent of macaroni and cheese along with pork chops hit him instantly. Grams looked over at them before smiling.

"Grams," Beau said, striding forward.

"It may not be my house, Beauregard, but get that hat off your head."

"Yes, ma'am." He swiped it off and ducked to kiss her cheek.

She harrumphed and wiped her hands off on a towel. "Anabelle Lee, you get in here and keep an eye on these chops while I meet this young lady."

Anabelle listened although Ethan knew she wasn't pleased by it. No one argued with Grams. His grandmother approached and, after a slight hesitation, reached and pulled Rally in for a hug. Ethan released her hand as she was held tight by Grams. She muttered something too low for him to hear as she rubbed Rally's back.

"It will all be better now, baby. Trust me. You've got one of the best watching out for you. These other two are the rest of the best. They'll make sure you make it home and back to your family. Now, where do you live? Have you told them you're alive?"

"Grams," Ethan interjected.

"What?"

"This is Rally. We haven't located her family yet."

Anabelle and Beau both sent him a look he knew to mean when the truth came out, they weren't protecting his ass from Grams for lying to her.

"Rally? You youngsters with your hip-hop names. Well, anyway, you're a beautiful woman and once we get some more meat on your bones, you'll be bringing the guys in from miles around." She slipped her arm through Rally's and led her to the kitchen.

Ethan didn't want to think of others around her.

"Now, I hope you like pork chops," she said as they moved away.

Beau and Anabelle Lee came to his side, putting him in the middle. "She's already matchmaking," Beau said.

Their phones alerted and they looked down at them. "When do you leave?" Ethan asked.

"Wheels up in three hours, the plane is inbound." Anabelle walked off and put her phone to her ear as she talked to someone.

Ethan wanted to go but he knew he wasn't in any shape to do that. Besides, he had Rally to think about.

"Where are you going?" he questioned.

"Middle East."

"Be careful."

"Come eat," Grams ordered, breaking off any further discussion on the subject. "You as well, Anabelle Lee. You know I don't allow phones at my table."

Nothing beat his grandmother's cooking and they all ate, keeping the conversation light. Once they were finished, Beau headed off to do the shopping and as Ethan cleaned up with Anabelle, Rally vanished and he assumed she'd gone to lie down. His family could get a bit loud at times.

"I like her, Ethan," Grams said as she and Anabelle bundled up to leave. "Treat her right." She hugged him then left.

Alone in the house, he set his alarm and trotted downstairs to the bedrooms. She was in bed, curled up in a bunch of blankets. He flexed his hand on the doorframe a few times before entering the room and joining her on the bed. He slipped beneath the blankets and drew her close to him, not speaking, just holding her.

Rally relaxed into him as he held her. At first she'd been unsure what he was after but when all he did was hold her, she began to sink into him. She'd needed a bit of time by herself after dealing with their grandmother. A vivacious and special woman for sure, but it was a bit much for her who'd been in her situation.

She stared out of the window at the snow that continued to fall. Thick fat flakes making their way to the ground mesmerized her in a sense.

"Are you feeling okay?" His question was whispered.

"Tired and a bit stressed."

"Would you like me to leave?"

"No." She blurted out the word before she realized she'd done so. Being in his embrace soothed her.

"Okay. Are you warm enough? I can turn up the heat if you'd like."

She shook her head. "I like being wrapped up in blankets."

"I can tell." He put one leg under hers and his other on top so she was captured between him. "Are you remembering things?"

She didn't realize he'd known about that. "Flashes."

"Like?"

Despite his body heat and the numerous blankets, she still shuddered. "Water, sputtering, believing I was drowning. Except..." She pursed her lips.

"Except what?"

"It wasn't salt water."

"I'm not following."

"The water in my face that I was choking on wasn't salt water. Fresh."

"You don't think you were in the crash?"

His entire body vibrated with tension but he still remained gentle and soft with his touches on her.

"I know the plane went down. I'm just not sure it crashed."

"The reasoning?"

"When I woke in the cell, I had no injuries. They were all sustained later when I was beaten." She licked her lips. "But I had nothing prior to that. I was out of it and in a fog. I can't see it all clearly, but I remembered people around me, muttering and talking." She closed her eyes. "I don't know. Maybe it was all a dream and I woke to the nightmare."

"My boss wants to talk to you."

She wanted to refuse but he'd done so much for her. "Okay."

"I don't want to rush you but he'd like to as soon as you feel up to it."

She wouldn't ever feel up to it but she'd done a lot of appearances when she'd not felt up to it before. "I'll make myself available whenever he wishes to speak to me."

"There's a princess answer if ever I've heard one."

His breath skimmed along her skin, making her think thoughts she needed to stay far away from. It wasn't working. This man, so close against her. His hands were close, if he just inched them up a bit they would be on her breasts.

Would he pinch her nipples? Suck them? Hold them tenderly? She whimpered and shoved the thought far from her mind.

"Despite it all, I am a princess," she said, admitting it for the first time in years.

"I know. I wouldn't be allowed to hold you like this if you were home, would I?"

"We wouldn't be allowed in the same room without a few guards around. Touching, definitely off-limits."

"I'm glad you're here then and not there."

So was she.

"Can I ask you something else?"

She was falling asleep. "Yes."

"Are you ready to call me by my name yet?"

This time there was no ignoring the longing that hit her. She easily recalled him saying if she used his name he would know she was ready for a real kiss.

"Ethan!" Beau shouted down. "Masters is in your den waiting to talk to Rally."

"Of course the fucker is," he muttered. "Ready to meet my boss?"

How did he get here when she'd just been asked if she would speak with him? "No but that's never stopped me before."

"I'm glad to see some of your spunk is coming back." He kissed her behind the ear and rolled free of the bed before reaching out a hand for her.

She gained her feet and checked her outfit.

"You're fine," he assured her. "Masters wants answers. He wouldn't care if you were naked. I would, but he wouldn't."

"You've already seen me naked."

A glint appeared in his eyes. "Not how I want you and not nearly long enough." He stepped back and gestured for her to leave the room.

More of that tingling shot through her as she preceded him from the room. She couldn't help herself from peeking in as they bypassed the open door. She shuttered her expression and yanked her gaze from there. It wasn't any of her business.

Hand on the baluster, she started up. "If you want to see my room, princess, all you have to do is go in there."

It wasn't fair how his voice affected her, creating this need in her gut—a need she wasn't sure she'd ever be able to resolve. At the top, he placed his hand on her back and guided her to a room she'd not been in before.

The man standing at the window was tall—taller than Ethan and wider. Sure, he'd not been held prisoner but his frame was all around more than Ethan's. Not that he was fat—he wasn't by any means—but he was definitely imposing.

He wore a black suit and turned when she entered. His dark features were expressionless as he glanced over at her. She stiffened her spine, forcing herself to recall she wasn't a prisoner but a princess. Against another wall was Beau and he gave her a smile and wink, which calmed her nerves a bit.

"You are looking better," he said, stepping forward.

That statement indicated Ethan's boss had seen her prior to this. She clasped her hands along her stomach.

"I have some questions for you."

She gazed about the room and picked a couch near the windows and sat on it, back straight and ankles hooked as she'd been trained to do.

"What do you remember?"

Ethan appeared at her side and placed a bottle of water within reach. She'd not known he'd slipped out—her attention had been on the man he called boss. Rally caught him up on what she'd told Ethan.

Masters stepped to the table and pressed a button. The wall to her left changed from the four pictures to computer screens. "Does any of this look familiar?"

She pushed up and moved to where she had a direct line of sight to them. "They look like jungle."

"You said you were taken to Venezuela. Do you have any idea where from? Or how long you were at the first place?"

She shook her head, staring at images of the heated rainforest. A chill skated up her spine. "No. Like I told Mr. Jackson, everything is just in flashes."

"What about the men who held you? Any names that you can recall?" He put up more faces. "Or any of these look familiar?"

She stared at the thirty-two faces he put up on the screens, eight per. One ticked her memory banks and she went closer to see if a better look would tell her one way or the other.

The screen she focused on flashed and there were only two faces per screen, larger and easier to stare at. Cocking her head to the side, she pointed at the top left.

"He's familiar. Not completely but there is something about him that makes him familiar to me."

That one's face was the sole one up there.

"Are you sure, Rally?" Ethan's voice was hard.

"Yes," she replied, turning. Ethan and Beau both sported serious scowls. "His eyes and nose. The mouth isn't all what I remember but he looks like someone I've seen previously. Not sure where but of the ones you posted he's the only one."

"It can't be," Beau said, walking toward Masters. "That bastard is —"

"Dead. Yes, I know Beauregard."

"Trevor Mansfield." Ethan crossed his arms and blew a frustrated breath. Beau had told him about Lexy's troubles and the shootout in Central Park that culminated in Trevor's death. "It is possible. She's been a prisoner for over three years. She easily could have seen him."

"Mansfield was a homegrown terrorist. Why would he be out in Venezuela or wherever else they had her?" Masters rested his hands on the table. "Anything else you recall about him?"

"No, sorry." She headed back for the couch when she stopped and pivoted. "I remembered water that wasn't real and the sound of metal." She shrugged. "I know it's not much in the way of help."

Chapter Six

Ethan tried to make sense of what she'd said. *Water that wasn't real? What the fuck does that mean?* From the lines in Beau's forehead, Ethan knew he was trying to reconcile what she'd stated as well.

"You're the only survivor we've had from any of these plane crashes," Masters said, his tone remarkably gentle and un-Masters-like. "Anything you can assist us with would be greatly appreciated."

Ethan cocked a brow at his cousin as she moved back closer to Masters and stared at the images on the table. Beau strode to his side.

"What do you make of this?"

"I don't know. I can't even think of where to begin with water that wasn't real." He kept his gaze on her, listening with half an ear as she spoke with Masters. Again noting how her body language had her more than a bit relaxed around his boss. A man most felt to be over-the-top imposing.

"What about hypnotizing her?"

"No way."

"Why not? We both understand the answers are buried in her mind. It's not a shock that, given what she went through, her mind's hidden them from her. We could bring them out."

"And plunge her directly back into the mindset of where she was before we got her out of there? You don't get it, Beau. *I* was losing my shit. I can't even begin to image what it was like for her."

"She's a lot stronger than you're giving her credit for."

"Doesn't mean I want to submerge her back into the memories."

"We need to know what's going on."

She tucked some hair behind her ear and nodded at something Masters said. "I know," he replied. "But give her a bit more time. Memories are cropping up and I'd rather she come by them on her own."

"She means something to you."

He couldn't deny it so he said nothing.

"Well fuck," Beau muttered. "Do you know what you're doing? Christ, Ethan. She's a princess."

"I'm aware of that. I'm just some common nobody."

"Not even going there. You're part of a clandestine organization and she's a *princess*. How exactly do you see this working out? The press would be digging all into your life, there would be paparazzi following you around."

Ethan shrugged. "Didn't say anything was going to happen."

Beau snorted. "Of course it will. You're a Jackson and a man who has his sights set on the woman he wants."

"I'm not an animal," he muttered.

"You're starting to sound like a man in love."

He shook his head. "I'm not in love. I don't know her that well."

"That is true. I mean, she almost never talks to you. But even after you threatened to kill her, dragged her away from that even though you could barely stand on your own, where—if I'm getting this recollection right—she saved your life, you bring her here to your fucking fortress in Georgia instead of sending her home. You've coded her into your alarm system and periodically check on her even when she's sleeping. Even now, standing here, you can't keep your eyes off her. I'd stand by a pretty confident assumption you're in love with her."

"We've both shared an experience."

"Will be sharing more, I wager."

"Not everything is about fucking, Beau."

His cousin laughed. "I never said anything about that, although I'm all for a willing woman in my bed. I meant overall."

"Don't you have a woman to fuck waiting in the wings?"

"Always, man, always one or two."

Ethan rolled his eyes. "Not needing to hear that."

"You asked." He sobered. "Seriously, Ethan, I don't want you hurt and you know if you pursue this, it will happen. Then your sister will go after her and that will not put her in good graces with the royal family."

"Oh, so if she does that, she's *my* sister?"

"Yes." His response was instant. "I claim her when she's not destroying the royal family."

They stopped talking when the entrance was filled by Mino who carried in a stack of files. She paused and looked at them. "Good to see you up and around, Ethan. Beauregard." Then she moved on to the table where she entered the conversation with Masters and Rally.

"How did she get in here?"

"She's been in here, just in the living room putting together whatever she just brought in. You know Masters travels with her now." Beau faced his cousin.

"Odd he does. She's important to him."

"Yes." Beau shared a look with him. "Should we go find out what they're talking about?"

"Yes."

Together they walked over there as Mino stepped away and began putting some maps up on the walls. Ethan positioned himself across from Rally although he frowned when Beau stood right beside her.

"I managed to pull the listings of anything related to Trevor Mansfield and they are marked on the maps." Mino dusted off her hands as she walked back to the table. "I gave you all the coordinates on the crashes so you can mark them on the computer."

Masters did that and they popped up, all around Asia. Remote locales.

"You ran all his aliases?"

"I may just be a secretary, Beauregard, but I know how to do my job." She glared at him.

Ethan looked at Rally who was staring up at the map on the screen. Edging around the table to her side, he stared at her. "What are you thinking, Rally?"

"Just wish I could remember more." She gave him a small smile that had the effect of cannon fire going off next to him.

"It will come back."

"You're not a normal guy, are you?"

He lifted one eyebrow. "I'm not?"

"No." She never allowed her gaze to waver from his. "All of this technology and everyone in the room. You're more."

He leaned closer, positioning his mouth by her ear. "You're right, I am more. Ready to say my name yet?"

Her gaze riveted on his mouth when he pulled back but she didn't speak. At least not until Beau called her attention. He watched them together — she didn't lean away from him as if she were worried or disliked him.

Anger unfurled in his gut when his cousin kissed her cheek, eyes on him. "I'm out of here. Y'all kids be good now." Then he walked out.

A mission. One he couldn't go on. He didn't like that feeling.

Back at the table he rejoined the conversation. Ten minutes later, he looked around for Rally and found her sleeping on the couch. Mino met his gaze and moved to cover her with a blanket before getting back to the talk.

"Do you want to send teams to the sites?" he asked.

"No. With the currents in the ocean, the debris will have moved. And with the massacre in Venezuela, there's nothing to do to figure out if any of them were the survivors. They were so mangled and burned there's not any way to learn identities. The few we did were local tribesman from the area."

"Right, so whoever is behind it cleaned up after himself and killed everyone to keep us in the dark. Making sure we couldn't learn anything."

"Yes."

"One thing I can't figure," Masters said.

"Only one? Because I'm confused as fuck." Ethan raked his hand through his hair.

"She's royalty, right? Wouldn't there have been guards with her? A protective detail? And why didn't she see any of them after she'd been captured? Do you think she was the sole survivor from the crash, if that's what happened?"

Another glance to the sleeping woman. "I don't know." He turned his attention to the in-screen keyboard. "I did think of something else, though."

"Which is?" Masters looked up at the four displays on the wall.

"You can bring down a plane and not leave a trace that it was tampered with. You just have to log in to the electrical systems and have it near the black box so when it goes down it basically overwrites the data in the box. So if, and I do mean if, it was recovered when the details were pulled up, it would show them on course and not where the plane had truly gone down."

"So someone had to be on the plane to do that?"

"Not at all. If it was installed prior, they could be thousands of miles away and do this."

"What if they didn't install it? I mean, could there be something out there capable of hacking into any plane's system?"

He nodded solemnly. "Yes, it's possible. Would have to be able to emit a strong signal and have a crack hacker, but it could be done."

"Well, fuck. That made a whole lot of other possibilities."

Ethan agreed with his boss. This could be catastrophic.

* * * *

"Are we ready?" he asked, walking up to the chair and placing his hands on the back while the person seated hovered their fingers over the keyboard.

"Yes, sir. Just awaiting your order."

He smiled and chewed on the cigar in his mouth. "Good, good. Make it so. Let's deprive the world of another plane."

"Yes, sir."

"Bring this one down over North Korea. No one will be investigating that, for he won't allow anyone in."

Lean fingers flew over the keyboard and the man pressed the final button and sat back. "Done."

"Wonderful. Now, I want to move prisoners from here to the new facility in Montevideo."

"At once. They'll be gone before sunset."

"Wonderful. When you're done, come to my room. I have *something* to discuss with you."

He dragged his hand along the man's neck, liking how he trembled. He would be doing so much more before the night was over.

"Yes, sir."

Pivoting on his heels, he walked out, a light whistle on his lips. Back in his room, he turned on the news and waited for it to hit the airwaves about the plane crash. When it did, he smiled and reclined, lacing his hands behind his head.

"Damn good day, if I do say so myself."

* * * *

Rally stood in the living room, a roaring fire to her back as she stared out of the window. She'd woken in a cold sweat with a scream on her lips. Years of swallowing them was the only reason it hadn't slid free.

Unable to sleep, she'd come upstairs and stood close to the fire until her chill had been banished. Then she'd moved to the window and enjoyed the glow of moonlight on the snow.

According to Ethan, more snow was supposed to fall. A lot of people were in a panic because of this weather. She was glad to be inside and not sleeping out in it.

"Everything okay?"

His smooth voice was like honeyed tea over her skin. She rubbed her arms. "Couldn't sleep."

He stood behind her and wrapped his arms around her. "Another nightmare?" He rested his chin on her head.

"Yes. Do you get them?"

"Every night."

Somehow that made her feel a bit better. Relaxing into him, she allowed him to be there with her. Her feelings for him were not leveling out but growing. Too fast. She knew there wasn't a future for them but she couldn't stop those thoughts.

"Want to talk about it?"

"No. I want them to stop."

"We both do, sweetheart. Mine are about the rats — all those damn rats — that would bite me. Not about the torture but the rats. Which in itself was a form of torture. I hate those things. When I first got there I would fight them off but as time continued, I had to conserve my energy."

"I'm sorry for what you went through."

"Why were you in the room that day?"

"I don't know. Rolf pulled me from my usual chores and wanted me to hold the tray. He'd been hinting for a while to have me in on — what he called — a true torture session. He liked to scare me."

"You were free. Why didn't you leave?"

"I did twice. The first time he whipped me until I could hardly walk. The second time, he shot a little girl in the head right in front of me and said it was because I had tried to run. And if I ever attempted to again, he would kill at least two. Perhaps more."

"A little girl? There were kids there?"

"Yes. They captured tribal women and raped them, had the kids running around. They were good to be lowered into small crevices to pick certain items. And expendable. If they died, well, he always said he could make more babies. They didn't matter."

He turned her into his chest and she rested her cheek against the warmth of his skin.

"The fucker used your caring to his advantage."

"I love children. It broke my spirit more than any of the beatings could have done. And I stayed."

"And he used the children any time he wanted leverage against you."

"I'm not sure why, I hadn't any clue of where I was or how to get home."

He stroked his hands up and down her back. Her heart sped as she soaked in his strength.

"Do you think he knew you were a princess?"

"Definitely. He called me princess. I suppose he never intended to ransom me or send me home."

He smoothed a callused palm against the small of her back and she whimpered at the electric touch. He didn't stop or speed up, just maintained the same easy motion. She tipped her head back and found him staring down at her, the moonlight casting his face in shadows. The harsh angles and chiseled features made him so handsome, she wanted to touch him and learn how it felt beneath her palm.

"You *are* free now," he whispered.

"Ethan." His name tumbled from her lips seconds before he captured them with purpose and confidence.

Rigid for all of two seconds, she melted against him, opening beneath his quest. Life pumped into her, making all the dark from her past three years fall away. Replacing fear with desire, despair with hope, and disgust with need. She curled her fingers along his sides, accepting the feel of his skin beneath her touch.

His kiss was masterful yet gentle. He searched her mouth, taking his time and exploring everywhere he could. As their tongues slid along each other, it made her nipples tighten as her clit throbbed with each passing second. She pushed up on her toes, wanting, *needing*, more contact with him.

To her surprise, he set her away from him. She was unable to read anything in his eyes.

Mortification swamped her. *How could I have been so foolish as to think he'd actually want anything like that from me?* Covering her mouth with one hand, she bolted. Dashed by him and ran downstairs to the bedroom he'd given her, ignoring his cry of her name.

How will I face him again? She crawled into bed and burrowed deep beneath the blankets, covering herself except for a small hole around her face.

One second she was alone and the next the bed dipped as he settled himself beside her. "Why did you run?"

"Leave me alone."

"Rally, talk to me."

She closed her eyes and shook her head. "I'd rather not talk about it."

"Fine, then listen. Don't think I stopped the kiss because I don't want you. I stopped it because I *do* want you."

That doesn't make the slightest bit of sense.

He stretched out on the bed, burying below the bedding as well until he pressed against her back. Wrapping an arm around her, he placed his hand on her stomach, below the shirt she wore. Again, his touch and the calluses did weird things to her insides.

"I don't understand."

"You're a princess."

She rolled her lower lip in her teeth before readjusting so they lay chest to chest. "And that means I'm off-limits."

His tongue dragged along his lower lip before he nodded slowly. "You're supposed to be."

"What happens now?" She didn't move away from him, not wanting to lose the warmth of his hand on her.

"I make that my mantra and do my best to stay away from you." His words were low and vibrated in her belly.

"You're sending me home?"

He flexed his fingers along her side. "No. You don't want to go. I'll keep you here."

"Because you want me around when my memory comes back."

A glint appeared in his eyes that not even the darker room could hide. "If that's what you need to tell yourself."

She bit the inside of her lip and sucked in a deep breath. "Stay?"

"I'll be right here."

Rally shut her eyes and willed sleep to come. Mentally and physically exhausted from the day of meeting with the big man named Masters. Trying to figure out what she was missing to help them had stressed her. But right here and now, she wanted some rest. A time where her thoughts were allowed to be peaceful and not reminders of what she'd gone through.

Three years. She couldn't get past that. She'd been gone for a long time.

Chapter Seven

Ethan typed on the clear keyboard, the fireplace offering up the only light to the room aside from the screens. He'd pulled everything he could about the princess who'd come into his life. The information he'd gotten on the plane had whetted his appetite about her. Now that he had his system, he wanted to know all he could.

Rally was asleep in her room. He'd woken about an hour ago and, unable to fall back asleep, had come over here. Some nights he slept with her. Others he waited until she went under then left, unable to sleep himself. They both still had nightmares and she occasionally would have terror sweats. Not that he didn't.

Her full memory still hadn't returned. Sure, some glimpses, but nothing concrete. The snow had gone, but it had been replaced by another storm that had covered the region with more and set the locals into a panicked uproar.

By all accounts this princess loved to buck the rules. She didn't respect the men who'd been assigned to protect her. In pictures or video clips there was always this rebellious expression on her features. As if she was about to make some large faux pas and embarrass her family.

However, despite it all, she hadn't ever. She'd attended dinners and speeches, but had made no qualms about hiding her beliefs. Where women and men should be treated equal. Rich or poor. He admired that about her.

A picture on the screens grabbed his attention and he rose from his seat to approach the wall. She stood among a group but appeared entirely alone. The purple dress draped her like a lover, accentuating each curve. This woman was a princess, haughty, regal. Stunning.

But there was something else. One of the men in the photo with her hit his memory and had him pausing. He watched Rally with an intensity that set Ethan's teeth on edge.

Even so, his gaze drifted back to Rally. Her entire body gave off a 'no touching' vibe and he could tell, despite there being nothing on her face that said it, she wanted to be anywhere else but where she was.

"Who are you?" he asked, tapping his cheek with one finger. "And why do you look familiar to me?"

Back by the keyboard, he homed in on the face and pushed it through the facial recognition software. He padded to the fridge and grabbed himself a beer. Popping the top, he stared out of the window as he drank. There was more snow falling. He returned to the room and checked the progression. No luck so far.

Seated on his couch, he picked up the receiver from the base and dialed a number. As expected it was answered on the first ring.

"What do you have?"

"Found a man in one of the pictures that rings a bell to me, but as of this moment, I haven't been able to ID him. Sending the image to you. I'm not sure if it's my memory that doesn't want to remember because of my time in Venezuela but maybe you will recognize him before the facial rec does."

"Going to my email now."

He pushed some buttons and sent the image. Lord help him, he longed to ask what he knew of his cousins, but he wasn't about to do that.

"Which one?" Masters asked.

"The dark-haired one watching her. A bit off to the side." He lifted his sight back to the image on the screens. More of that tingling hit him and he swore as the room spun. Shaking it off, he set his bottle down and pushed to his feet. Every few steps he stopped and glanced around him, expecting rats to be on him.

"Ethan?"

Masters snapped him back to the fact he had the phone in his hand. "What?"

"What's going on? Are you okay?"

"Yes, just a bit dizzy. Let me know if you figure out who it is." He ended the call and dropped the phone to the table he walked by.

His skin burned and he couldn't shake the belief there were vermin running up and down his body, biting and clawing at him. He strode to the front door, shoved his feet into his boots, and stepped outside into the night.

The cold. Perhaps it would be better if he froze them off. He headed down the steps, turned left at the landing, and hit the ground running. In the woods, he began scrubbing snow on his exposed skin. No matter how much snow he covered himself with he still burned with the pain they inflicted.

More. He needed more chill. Eventually they would leave him alone. On his knees, he gathered as much snow as he could, pulling it toward him to use as a cover. A low keening cry left him as he rocked forward allowing the accumulating snow to be his blanket.

* * * *

"No," he said, pushing away the person shaking him.

"You have to wake up." More shaking resumed.

"No." Waking up meant facing more torture. He wanted it to end. "If you're going to kill me, do it and get it over with."

"I need you to wake up."

That voice was different. Feminine and one that created a protective emotion in him. Women were to be safeguarded.

Still he fought it, submerging himself in the cold that hugged him so securely.

"I'm scared, Ethan. I can't move you by myself."

Her sentence brought his eyes open. He pushed up from the ground, taking in the state of undress he was in. Pants and boots. Not smart for being out in the snow. Turning to the left, he found Rally crouching there, wearing his coat, and watching him with wide eyes.

"Do I want to know what I'm doing out here like this?"

"I don't know." She rose. "I found the front door open and followed your tracks. Found you like this."

He'd sleepwalked a few times but this was crazy. He reached for her hand, took it and drew her up to her feet. "Let's get back inside."

His mind raced as they walked. He entered the code at the door and had her enter first. Following, he grimaced when the heat hit him. He glanced at the clock and noticed he'd been outside for nearly two hours.

"You should get warmed up."

He dipped his head to glance at the woman beside him. He released her with a nod. "Right."

She shrugged out of the coat and hung it on the coat rack. Ethan gripped the back of her sweatshirt as she started by him for the stairs.

"Thank you," he said. "For coming after me."

For a brief second he believed she was going to say something but she didn't, instead walking away to disappear downstairs. After a moment, he followed suit and entered his bedroom to shower.

Finished with that, he went back to the room to check on the progress of the recognition. There was a cup of warm tea waiting for him as he entered. He scoured the room but there was no one there.

He perched on the edge of his couch and rubbed his temples. His worlds of reality and fantasy were merging. Stuff didn't make sense anymore. What was he going to do about it? Tell Masters? No, that would result in him heading for therapy.

"What are you looking for?"

Rally stood in the doorway, as if she were waiting for permission to enter. He beckoned her in and she quietly came toward him. Ethan took her hand and laced their fingers together. Pressing a kiss to the back of her hand, he tugged her to sit beside him.

This he could focus on. Work. Not whatever messed-up fucking crap rolled around in his head.

"I'm running a search for the man in the picture there. The one watching you. Do you know him?"

He observed her reaction as she looked up to the screens. She blinked a few times then canted her head to the side. Something rang a bell but he wasn't sure if she knew him or not.

Rally stared at the image, more unease slithering up her spine like a black mamba as it moved over the ground. "Where did you find that picture?"

"Do you recognize it?"

His thumb never stopped as he rubbed against her hand. She enjoyed the feel of his touch.

"Yes. Where did you get it?"

"In some old files online. Why?"

"This... This was a private function. There weren't supposed to be any cameras at this event."

"What event is it?"

"This was..." She worried her lower lip. There were some things which were best kept among family. "Something private."

He released her. "Do you know the dark-haired man watching you? The only one who isn't paying attention to the rest of the things going on? Instead he's focused on you."

Lord, she wanted to clam up. "I know him. We called him Axel Frost."

"Called?"

"He was at the palace a few times, but about a month after this, he stopped showing up. I never saw him again. Do you know him?"

"He's familiar to me. Something about him tells me I've met him before. I just can't put my finger on it." She watched his long fingers move along the keyboard. "I don't know the name Axel, however. Running it now. What did he do? And why are you ignoring what the event was?"

She stiffened. "If I wanted to tell you what it was, I would have said something other than it was private."

He turned his head toward her with the speed of molasses. "You're sounding more and more like a princess."

"As you pointed out, I am one." She rose and walked closer to the image.

He followed her. "What about this makes you not pleased to be there? It's obvious you want to be anywhere but where you are."

Professional expression. Detached. That's how she would explain her features. It wasn't something she had forgotten, not even now. "The life of royalty isn't always glamorous. Especially in my family." She hoped there'd be enough finality in her tone for him to drop it. She should have known better.

"I need to know what that event was so I can find this man. It isn't any coincidence that he was watching you that hard. Was he a suitor of yours?"

"A suitor?"

Ethan met her gaze as he returned to his computer. "Yes. Asking for your hand in marriage. Trying to become part of the family."

She lifted her shoulders, suddenly freezing despite the warmth in the room. "Perhaps. I wouldn't have known about it until the wedding if he was in negotiations with my father or not."

He stilled. "Negotiations?"

She dug deep for the cold shell she'd had around her for so long, the one that had served her well while she'd been before the press and other royalty. It wasn't easy. Her time in captivity had pretty much destroyed all of it. "I'm property. Something to further someone's ambitions. I'm traded, bartered and offered for."

"Jesus," he uttered. "That's a cold way of looking at who you may spend the rest of your life with."

"It is our way." She thought back to the few times Axel had been there. He had been interested in her but, as she did with most people her father wanted her to interact with, she kept him at as much of a distance as she could. There wasn't any reason in her mind to make anything easy for him.

"This way you would have no way of knowing if this man was even compatible for you?"

"That has nothing to do with it." She refocused on the screen, taking in Axel's dark looks. He had green eyes and tan skin from being out in the sun so much. "It's about what each side can gain."

"Without care to what happens to you?"

"My emotional state is less than his next deal." She held no illusions about how she was viewed. It had been ingrained in her from the beginning. However, as she'd gotten older and had begun speaking out, she'd found that to be her outlet. Help others despite the fact that the person she longed to help the most was herself, and she couldn't.

"That's fucking bullshit."

She shuddered as more goosebumps popped up on her skin. Moving to the window, she stared out over his property. She'd woken alone and frightened because of another nightmare. Slipping from bed, she'd gone looking for him. However, now that they were back inside she couldn't escape the chill.

She rubbed her throat then turned to look at Ethan. He drank the tea she'd made for him as he continued furiously on the computer. On silent feet, she headed out of the door and back down to the room she'd been given.

Lying back on the bed, once again buried deep beneath the thick blankets, she squeezed her eyes shut. Who was Axel to Ethan and what could she remember about the man to maybe assist him in locating his whereabouts?

She didn't remain on Axel. Her mind flashed her back to the prison. Over and over on an endless loop, all she could see was the little black-haired girl being shot.

She whimpered, refusing to give in to the cries. Yet it never ceased. Again. And again. And again. Her small body, crumpled to the ground, blood everywhere.

"Shh."

Through her fog of fear and terror, Ethan's voice reached her. She started and his arms tightened around her waist.

"I'm right here, princess."

She bit her lip so hard the metallic taste of blood filled her mouth. He rubbed her chilled skin, sharing his heat with her.

"I don't feel well," she said.

"As in you want to sleep or as in you're about to puke all over this bed."

"Both."

He climbed out and brought her a bucket. Then he slipped back in behind her. "You're burning up." He swiped a hand along her forehead. "I think I need to get you to a doctor."

His words faded as she succumbed to the darkness waiting for her. The next few times she became lucid for a moment—all she heard was beeping. The room was otherwise dark. When she finally opened her eyes and found someone in there, she recognized Mino.

"I see you're awake finally. This is a good thing. I'm going to get Ethan." She left the room and true to her word was back with him in short order.

He hurried to her side and sat on the bed with her. Smoothing his hand along her face, he smiled. "You had me worried, princess."

"How long have I been lying here?"

His expression tensed for a moment before he responded. "You've been out for almost a week."

"What happened?"

"Dehydration and you still had some fungal-viral thing inside you that wasn't ready to give you up yet."

Rally didn't have any fight left in her so she closed her eyes once more and allowed the exhaustion to take center stage.

Chapter Eight

"She had a what?" Ethan scratched the back of his head as he stared at Mino who sat at his kitchen counter on a bar stool.

Mino glanced at him then Masters before stirring her tea, adding some honey, then stirring it even more. "My contact said it was a derivative of African Trypanosomiasis." She shrugged. "He couldn't explain why it manifested the way it had or where she'd picked it up, especially given how she'd been in South America for the past few years."

He snapped his gaze to her face. "You told him about her?"

Mino held up her hand. "Can it. I've worked for Theta Corps long enough to know what all I can and can't say." The door opened and in walked his sister and cousin. She looked at them for a mere second before meeting his eyes again. "I gave him a hypothetical, telling him about the symptoms and a broad overview of what the situation was." Her lips lifted slightly. "He assumed I was heading back to medical school and was in the process of working out an idea for a thesis."

"Boyfriend?" Anabelle Lee asked as she walked to the fridge.

Mino's offhand shrug was symptomatic of something his sister would do. "Anyway, he did say if it was something where I had the opportunity to truly meet and study someone who'd gone through that, he would like to know. Perhaps even do some testing of his own."

Beauregard settled beside her and hooked his boot heel on the rung. "Any progress on her memory?"

Ethan ran a hand down his face. "We were talking about it when she suddenly walked out of the room. About a man named Axel Frost, or rather that's how she knew him. I recognize him as someone else, but whom or from where I can't ascertain. I'm still running it. Anyway," he said, ingesting some of his protein drink, "I headed back down to her room and found her in the throes of another nightmare. When I went to wake her, she was burning up." He exhaled and looked at everyone in there with him. "I don't know if I've been pushing her too hard. Or if it's all a coincidence and for reasons unknown she is reacting to something she picked up God knows where. Perhaps she was somewhere in Africa when they first took her. I just don't know. We've been home for a time now but her nightmares seem to be getting worse instead of better. Is that normal?"

"I'm not a shrink. I don't have a clue." Mino drank her tea. The others said much of the same thing.

Masters crossed his arms. "I can bring in someone for her to talk to if you'd like."

Ethan thought about it. Then he looked at his sister and cousin. In their eyes he saw the understanding of what he was about to decide. "No, I have someone."

"Good. When can I talk to her again?"

"Seriously, Masters?" Anabelle Lee snapped. "The woman is suffering from nightmares and you want to push her harder? You've always been a callous bastard but this takes the cake even for you, don't you think?"

Their boss looked at his sister, eyes narrowing. "I have a responsibility to the world, Ms. Jackson. If that means I have to push one woman in order to get the answers I need to stop people like the ones who are knocking planes out of the sky for no other reason than they can and want to, then I will."

"Sometimes if you don't push, you get what you want faster than if you do. Because all they get is angry and resentful of the strong-arm tactics."

"Odd coming from you, who despises coddling."

Ethan stared between them then looked over to where Beau and Mino also watched avidly.

"There's a difference between coddling and allowing someone the chance to remember on their own." Annabelle held Masters' stare without flinching.

Mino moved away. "I don't need to hear this." She left and Beau followed. Ethan looked at the arguing pair and took his drink and vacated the area as well. Instead of heading where Beau and Mino went, he opted to head back down to where he'd left a sleeping Rally.

He paused in the doorway of her room. She lay as still as death. The blankets over her were tucked up to her armpits. The light yellow color surrounded her like a warm ray of sun. Outside the large window, snow still fell in large fat flakes. The area was on lockdown and wasn't truly prepared for weather like this.

Her thick lashes were on her cheek, her color had begun to return and her breathing had settled down. Now she looked at peace. No nightmares. No fever. No anything but the wonderful world of sleep.

He closed his eyes and pinched the bridge of his nose. When he opened them, Rally was looking at him. A small smile lifted her lips.

"What's going on?"

"Nothing," he said easily. "Typical stuff going on up there. Family arguments, food. Masters."

"He has more questions for me, doesn't he?"

"I won't let him push you." He shifted against the doorframe.

She shook her head and sat, scooting back to lean on the headboard. "Push or otherwise, if what I know can help, then my nightmares and discomfort are irrelevant."

He sat beside her and gripped her face in his hand. "Never say that to me. Nothing about you is irrelevant." His tone had dropped to an arctic chill.

She fiddled with the coverlet and cleared her throat. "I'm ready to talk to him. I still don't think I will be of any assistance to him but I'm okay with trying again."

He lightened his grip and leaned close to kiss her gently. "Come up when you're ready." Then he departed the room. He jogged back up the stairs and stepped into the living room. "She's on her way."

"Good," Masters said, pushing to his feet, waving Mino to his side. "I need you to take care of this for me."

Ethan watched her reaction as she read the sheet. She wasn't pleased with what she saw but she nodded. "On my way."

"Drop me off at home?" Beauregard sauntered over to Mino.

"Sure." She folded the note into her pocket. Mino glanced at him. "Ethan."

He gave her a smile and replied, "Thanks for coming."

"All you have to do is call." She walked out, leaving Beau to follow. He saw a flash of red and watched his sister head out as well.

"I'm ready."

Ethan turned at the sound of Rally's voice. She stood there, hands clasped before her. The black flannel pants and dark blue sweatshirt hung off her frame, bringing his attention to how undernourished she remained.

Her hair draped over her right shoulder and his heart seized when she lifted her gaze to his. He strode to her and grasped her arm.

"Can I get you anything? Food? Drink?"

"I would prefer to get this over with, please." Her words were low and weak.

Glancing over his shoulder, he glared at Masters who once again sat. The man had no expression. On one hand, he understood his desire to push for answers to obtain results. However, this was Rally. The young woman who'd saved his life and who'd come to mean so much to him. Ethan's instinct was to protect her.

"It gets too much and we stop." He led her to the black leather love seat. Tugging her down beside him, he then tucked her close.

"Ethan said you were speaking German the other night. Before you got sick."

Her entire body tensed. Ethan flexed his fingers along her shoulder.

"I had no idea I was doing that," she murmured.

To him, it sounded as if the words were forced.

Masters leaned forward. "Any other memories?"

A shudder skipped along her slender frame. "A few. More flashes."

"And they were of?"

She played with the hem of her skirt. "Bars. Screams. Water that…"

"That what?" Ethan asked.

"I don't know how to explain it." She gestured around with her hands, making abstract motions. "I can't explain it yet. I did see where I was first. There were both mountains and beach." She licked her lips. "I remember smelling the ocean on the breeze." A ghost of a smile appeared before it was wiped away, replaced with a sadness that nearly broke what remained of his heart. "Warm. Not as humid like Venezuela. But warm." Another tremor. "At times it was arid."

Ethan met the steadfast gaze of his boss. Rally had again switched to German. She continued speaking, sky color. Clouds and descriptions of people that she'd seen.

When she broke for a drink, Ethan migrated to the window. Masters joined him.

"What do you think?" he asked his boss.

"Like you said, her memories are returning. The German bit is confusing. Not sure why that's what she's speaking."

"If that was all she heard, it makes sense."

"I get that but why now that she's safe? Is she still identifying with those who hurt her?"

"It's not Stockholm's." He growled the words.

"Never thought that. Just curious. I taped the conversation and am heading back to have Mino type it up. Do some cross-checking and go from there." He walked away two steps then paused, pivoting to look at Ethan. "How are you handling being back?"

He had no reason to lie to the man. "Not easy but I'm adjusting." Ethan rubbed the nape of his neck. "She woke me before she got sick."

Masters arched a brow.

"I'd walked out and lay on the ground in the snow. Only in my pants. Straight from bed. The rats... I always thought they would leave me alone if I could just manage to be in the cold. Guess on some level I still do."

"You need to see someone."

He gave a sharp shake of his head. "No. I'll work through it."

"See you do." Masters departed.

"Sure," he mumbled. "Because I've been having such rousing success thus far."

He went to find Rally. She stood in the kitchen, unmoving, staring down. Walking up behind her, he saw blood streaming from her hand mixing with the tomato juice from the slices she'd made.

"Shit. What the hell happened, Rally?"

He pried the knife from her unresponsive body and moved her hand beneath a stream of water. She sagged forward and he supported her as she shook her head.

"What's going on?" she asked.

"What a pair we make, princess," he said, pressing his lips to her temple.

* * * *

Unease arose in Rally as Ethan edged the truck up the driveway. She flexed the fingers on her injured hand. Tall trees lined the path they were on. The house wasn't as large as the one belonging to the man driving but it was cheery. Despite the gray cloudy sky, the yellow home radiated warmth and love. Smoke churned from the chimney. The porch was dotted with chairs.

"Grams thought it would be nice to spend some time with you."

"Why?" She didn't mean it to be rude but honest curiosity won out.

"I would love to have some grand reason but truth is, she is the boss. She dictates and we listen."

She couldn't imagine the other two related to him blindly listening to anyone. "All of you?" Dawning set in. "She raised you."

Affection spread along his features, softening the harsh lines. *Wonder what kind of man he was before Rolf got a hold of him. How many lives has the man ruined?*

Ethan parked the truck, unhooked his belt, and angled his body to her. Swirling in his eyes, she found the trust she had for him.

"Take this." He gave her a phone. "You call me if you need me. Voice activated, just tell it to 'call Ethan' and it will." He curved his strong fingers around her hand as he pressed it into her palm.

Panic blossomed. She figured it showcased on her expression for he slid one hand around and cupped the nape of her neck.

"You're not staying?"

"I have some things to do with Beau and Anabelle Lee. Some work. You'll be safe. But if you need me, call." He held her gaze, his own steadfast.

"What am I supposed to do?"

"Sit and visit. My grandmother wants to get to know you. Nothing more than that. Nothing less. She'll ply you with food and ask you about your family. She doesn't mean anything by it. It's her way." He swiped his finger along her jaw and thumbed her lower lip. "Do you want me to stay?"

Beyond him she spied his grandmother standing on the porch, a crocheted shawl around her shoulders. She desperately wanted to stay with him but accepted she had to find her own backbone and prepare to stand on her own without him as support.

"I'll be fine," she replied, staring down at her lap.

"Look at me, princess."

She obeyed. His gaze waited and she wanted to crawl against him, soak up his heat, and forget everything else around her existed.

"You'll be fine."

She nodded, trusting his words. His smile was swift with a hint of devil in it. He released her and climbed out. Offering back his hand, she took it after which she slid over the bench seat and landed beside him on the ground.

Side by side they walked to the porch. The woman there had a kind smile on her face.

"Ethan," she said, approaching with arms wide for a hug.

"Hi, Grams." He took the hug and wrapped his arms around her in return. He kissed her cheek. "How are you?"

"Missing my grandson."

"I know," he replied. "You remember Rally."

"Of course. Come here, chil'."

She listened and was enveloped in a hug of her own. These feelings were odd for her family didn't show affection like this even when she was home. They weren't like that. This, however, was nice.

"How are you settling in with my grandson?"

"He's been a very gracious host."

She blinked and looked at both of them before she laughed, head back and full-bodied. "Oh lawd. She's got more manners than you will ever have. I like her. Come on out of the cold."

Ethan followed them in and paused by the door. "I'll leave you two here so I can get over to Beau's."

"Go on. We'll be fine."

Rally shoved the unease down, put her hand in her pocket and curled it around the phone. Her lifeline to Ethan.

"Yes, ma'am," he said. His grandmother got another kiss then he was before Rally. He put his forehead to hers. "You'll be fine. I'm only a phone call away."

She nodded. "I know."

"Say my name so I can kiss you." His whispered words dragged along her skin like silk.

She couldn't. Not in front of his grandmother.

His grandmother clucked her tongue. "Ethan, leave that poor girl alone. We have talking to do."

"Saved. Fine. Save it for later. That way I can do more than kiss you."

Her blood burned and she averted her gaze. His chuckle heated her further. Ethan stepped away and walked to the door. "Have fun, ladies." The door clicked behind him.

"Let's start with something warm to drink and eat. Then we can talk and I can get to know the woman my grandson is determined to protect."

Rally trailed her into the spacious kitchen. The area was spotless but she could feel the love lingering in the air. It was nearly overwhelming but not in a bad way. Just one that she wanted to know more about.

"Sit."

She moved to the table and sat in one of the tall, dark chairs. Moments later, there was a steaming cup placed in front of her.

"Peppermint tea with honey." A plate of thick slices of bread were next. "Zucchini bread with chocolate chips, warmed up, and there's butter if you'd like to have some of that on it as well."

Taking one of the small plates, she lifted a piece of the bread. The scent filled her nose and her stomach clamored for a taste. She tore off a bite and popped it in her mouth. Moist and delicious.

"This is wonderful, thank you."

"You can call me Grams." The woman sat and plucked up a piece of her own after which she spread butter on it. "I have to thank you for saving my boy's life."

She sipped some tea and dabbed the corners of her mouth. "I didn't—"

"Yes, you did. I know you did. Beau told me." She sighed. "They think I don't know a lot of what they do, but it all is known to me. They've never been able to hide it, no matter how hard they try."

"He saved me as well." The words were true.

Indecision alive inside her, Rally dug deep for the smile she'd used numerous times before, in a life she'd long forgotten when she wanted to put someone at ease. Her father's teaching rang in her mind. *It's not about you. It is about making them feel better and they will come around to see it in your vision.* While she wasn't looking to get an angle on Ethan's grandmother, the smile was something she could fall on.

"Are you settling in well?" Grams asked, sipping her drink.

Sucking the moist crumb off her thumb, Rally nodded. "He's been nothing but the consummate gentleman."

Grams' eyes crinkled in the corners when she laughed. "That's a good one, honey. I know now you're not one of those empty-headed vessels he's usually around."

She flicked her eyes to the table and reached for her mug. The warm porcelain had a large white flower on the pale blue background. Beautiful.

"It's a magnolia." She jerked her gaze back over the table to Grams. The woman pointed at the mug. "That flower, it's a magnolia. Common around here."

"I bet they smell beautiful."

"They do. The trees lining the drive are all magnolias. My granddaughter painted this set."

"Anabelle Lee?"

"She doesn't strike you as a painter, does she? Well, she is one. Not often enough in my book does she pick up a brush, but when she does" — she tapped the vessel — "the results are amazing."

No, she did not picture the woman she'd first laid eyes upon clad in camouflage gear holding a gun as if it were an extension of her own body to be the kind of woman who created something so delicate and beautiful. "She's very talented."

"I know, I've always known that about her. But she had to follow in the boys' footsteps. Never wanted to stay in and do 'girly' things." She gave a strained smile. "I should get to work on dinner. You can tell me about you while we cook."

Rally finished up her bread before she realized she'd scarfed it down. Mortified that she had eaten as if it would be taken from her, she tentatively lifted her head. Grams had a smile on her face as she took the plate.

"Good, you ate it all. I hate to waste food. Bring your tea and you can help me. Ethan said you cut your hand, so we'll not have you putting any extra pressure on that."

Obediently, she listened. In moments, she was by the sink rinsing off the vegetables for the salad.

"You're very quiet for a woman who will be part of the family, young lady. You will have to learn to speak up or they will run all over you. It's how we are."

Rally almost dropped the peppers in her hand. Part of the family? She *had* to be hearing things.

"Yes, you heard me right. You're now part of this family."

"Stop trying to scare her, Grams."

Anabelle Lee's voice punctured Rally's bubble of rising panic. She yanked her gaze from the yellow vegetable in her hand and put it on the woman with vibrant red hair.

Trying? Oh, Rally had gone soaring past trying and was headlong in fear.

And Ethan's sister wasn't doing anything to help with the sharp looks she gave when Grams wasn't in sight. Rally understood her — she came across as being nice but there existed no doubt in her mind that this redhead equated with being one of the most dangerous people she'd ever met. She didn't view Anabelle Lee as a painter but how she'd seen her in the jungle, ready for death and destruction.

I should know better than to assume how some people are. I grew up surrounded by vipers along with those whose true faces were never known.

Chapter Nine

Ethan gripped the edge of the pool table and rocked forward. "Beats the fuck out of me, Beau. Some days I'm so pissed all I want to do is level everything in my path. Then there are days when I don't want to leave the bed."

His cousin lounged against the bar in his basement, fingers around a beer. "We'll find the fuckers who did this to you, Ethan. And when we do, they *will* pay."

"I know. I know all of that logically and yet I'm still..." He tipped his head back and stared at the light. "Not recovered."

"You've not been home that long, Ethan. You have to give yourself time."

"How much time? I'm a danger to everyone around me." He raked a hand through his hair and paced the perimeter of the table.

"You want me to put Rally elsewhere?"

His limbs locked as he went rigid. "Don't you dare." He forced the words from his chest where they came out a mixture of a warning and a promise of retaliation.

Nonplussed, Beau cocked an eyebrow. "You're the one who said you're a danger to everyone around you, not me."

"She stays with me."

"I figured as much." He rolled his shoulders. "If you're that worried about what you might do, how do you want to handle it?"

Ethan walked to the dartboard and pulled out the six embedded in the cork. "You know, I think about what I went through and how it's affecting me. Then I think about having been in a place like that for three years. I can't even begin to image what she went through." He backed up and threw the first two where they landed to the left of the bull's-eye.

"We all have different ways of coping, Ethan. She trusts you and that is helping her recover."

"What happens when I have to let her go home?" He threw again, making an adjustment so they landed dead center.

"That sounds a lot like you're asking for advice on relationships. I don't do them. I can't help you there."

"If I could just figure out this fucker Rolf and maybe get somewhere, then I could...argh! I feel so fucking useless. I can't go on missions and I can't do anything from this end. What good am I? I can't find this guy and if I can't..."

"He's a ghost. We know this but we also understand you have alerts set up to let you notify us if he's been located."

Ethan returned to the board and yanked out the darts again. "Everyone should have some sort of trail. This is insane."

"Another plane has gone down."

Ethan angled his head to take in his cousin. "What? When?"

"We just heard about it. They'd been keeping it quiet because of where it happened."

"And that would be?"

"Over North Korea."

"Shit," he uttered, striding for his laptop. "When did it happen?"

"A while ago. It's why we left. They're not allowing anyone in to check out the wreckage and are controlling all the news reports on the incident."

"Where was the plane from and where was it headed?" He flipped open his computer and brought it to life with the touch of a button. Darts beside him, he began trolling for information on it. Anything he could locate.

He knew Beauregard and Anabelle Lee had been over there, digging up what they could as well, lives in danger because North Korea didn't like outsiders in their country.

But if whoever brought the plane down there had been under the impression it would keep Theta Corps from searching into it, they were sorely mistaken. A feral smile turned up his lips. Doing this felt right down to his bones, it helped chase away the memories of his time as a prisoner.

He accepted the chair his cousin had slid over to him, not stopping his fingers from flying over the keyboard. He pulled up any information he could find on the plane's disappearance and sent it to the multiple screens in his room upstairs to be checked over later. Beau stole the darts from beside him.

"I will send you the information Masters recovered from our trip over there. Or call Mino and have her send it to you."

As the words fell from Beau's lips, Ethan sent an email to Mino requesting the information. Then he returned to digging for more snippets of information. Every so often he glanced at the time and tried to figure out how much longer he was going to be without Rally beside him.

Beau's laugh had him looking to his cousin. "What?"

"Just wondering how much more time will pass before you just give up and go get Rally from Grams' house. Of course then you have to explain to Grams why you can't leave her there for longer than an hour." His smile was pure evil. "Then I get to watch her lay into you. Haven't seen that in a while. It'll be fun."

"You really are an asshole."

Beau nodded. "Yes, yes I am." He pulled the darts free. "It's not like they're unprotected over there. Anabelle Lee is there."

"Not sure that's good or not. She isn't a fan."

"You're her brother—no one is going to be good enough for you." He stepped back and began throwing darts once more. "I'm more concerned about you."

He looked up from the computer to find that, despite his words, Beau hadn't turned from the darts. "How so?"

"Because of what you went through and because of Rally. You've already fallen for her and you know she has to go home."

He clenched a fist. "Not until there isn't any danger."

"She's a princess. There will always be danger around her. It's why she has bodyguards."

"Where the fuck were they?"

Beau angled toward him, eyes uncharacteristically kind. "She just remembers part of what happened. It's very possible the ones with her were killed or died in the crash. Yes, I'm aware it's also possible that they betrayed her, so you don't need to say it."

"Regardless, I'm not a prince."

"Not quite. Hillbilly and a redneck, sure. Prince. Nope."

"She saved my life." Beau nodded. "She trusts me." His cousin crossed his arms. "Damn it! I can't let her go, Beau. She stops my nightmares. I'm not ready to have them come back."

"I wish I could tell you it was going to get easier, but I can't. I wish I could make them go away, but I can't." The darts fell to the table. "I will tell you this—I will find the fucker responsible for this and I will be with you as the life leaves his body. We *will* get him, Ethan."

The conviction in his cousin's tone helped calm the raging beast within him. Ethan sighed heavily and accepted he would have to be patient a little bit longer.

* * * *

The buzzer woke him and he rolled to his left, reaching for the phone. "What?"

"He's here."

A thrill shot through his veins as he sat and swung his feet to the floor. "I'll be down in five minutes. Give him anything he wants."

"Yes, sir."

The call ended and he peered over his shoulder to the young man lying there, sound asleep. His cock stirred and yet he ignored his desire—the man waiting was more important than his need for relief. Naked, he walked to his large closet and drew on a pair of white linen pants, followed by a matching shirt. Shoving his feet into loafers, he then made his way to the door and walked out without looking back.

Exactly five minutes later, he pushed into the room where his guest waited. The man stood as he approached, his mixed heritage of Latin and Caucasian obvious. Tall, strong and fit, a thrill of a different kind rocketed through him.

"Thank you for coming, Carlos."

Every inch of Carlos screamed dangerous and for the first time, he was a bit nervous. The man ran his brown gaze over him.

"You offered me money, so I'm here. Before we get started, I want you to know if I agree to do this and you try to stiff me or fuck with me in any way, I will kill you, make what you do in your little camps in the jungle look like a theme park. Are we clear? I know who you are, your family, and I will wipe every trace of your line off the face of the planet." He leaned back in the chair and curved tan fingers around the glass beside him. "You don't and we'll get along fine."

"Point taken. I can live with that."

The gaze upon him was no warmer than ice. "So what's the job?"

"Do you know this man?" He slid a picture of Ethan over the coffee table.

Square, clean nails tipped the long fingers reaching for the image. A twitch in the jawline was the only indication there had been any reaction at all.

"Ethan Jackson. Yes, I know him."

"He took something of mine and I want it back."

His visitor moved his gaze from the picture to him. "Something?" *A bit of interest there.*

"More aptly, some*one*. I want her returned to me."

"Who is this person?" Back to monotone.

"She's a princess, and she's mine. I'm holding her for a while."

"And Ethan's family? Are his cousin and sister around?"

"Have you met them?"

"Yes. That's why I am asking. Ethan himself is formidable. But if his family is there, that is even more and will cost more."

"What do you want? I've already agreed to your astronomical price."

"No, not money. I want Ethan's sister."

Definitely emotion this time. *Such a shame. He would be one hell of a man to take to bed. I'd even be willing to bottom for him. Have him fuck me while I'm fucking Zahra. That would be perfect. Or have her blowing me while he fucks me. So many versions of how this could play out.* "Take her. I don't care if you kill her or fuck her. I just want my princess back and that Ethan bastard brought to me so I can kill him at my leisure."

"Deal. I'll bring you Ethan and the princess and I get Anabelle Lee."

"Who is she to you?"

Brown eyes narrowed. "Who is Princess Zahra Kidjo to you, Axel Frost?"

The man hadn't been kidding—he did know who he was. "She is going to be my wife." He didn't blink. "And to you, Carlos? If we're putting all the cards on the table, who is the sister?"

His grin set the hair on Axel's neck up in alarm. "Anabelle Lee is *my* ex-wife."

* * * *

"This is beautiful." Rally stared at the quilt resting on the chair.

"Thank you. I'm making it for Ethan. I think he needs one in his life." Grams took her seat then Rally took hers. After years of being seated first, having been prisoner, she had changed and always waited. "Do you quilt?"

"No, ma'am."

"You should, it's relaxing." She gestured to the basket of fabric. "Pick out something that speaks to you."

Rally bent at the waist and peered through all the different colors of material there. Also different types, some thin, some thicker, some softer. Toward the bottom, she found one that had her pausing.

"Found one you liked, I see."

Carefully, she brought it up to the top of the basket and held it to the light. The rich blue had soft gold threads running through it that danced in the sunlight. "It's stunning." More than just the look and feel of the material, something about it called to her, spoke to her.

Grams just hummed and continued quilting. "Anything else there you like?" She sewed by hand, not with a machine. Each square, however, looked perfect.

"What is this one?" She drew out a jean material one with a small green tractor on it.

"That's from Beauregard's pants when he was a boy. I could hardly get them off him to wash. Most of the material I quilt from has some sort of meaning to us."

"And this piece?" She held up the blue and gold one she'd picked.

"Ethan's baby blanket."

"Oh." Her fingers fumbled the material and she just about dropped it. "I see."

"So do I."

The door opened and Anabelle Lee entered, her skin ruddy from the cold. "Grams, I don't think we've ever had a winter like this one before. It's colder than —"

"You may be a grown woman, Anabelle Lee, but this is still my house," she interrupted. "You will mind your tongue when you speak. I didn't raise you to be crass."

"I was going to say colder than I could recall."

Grams didn't even look up. "Didn't raise you to be a liar, either."

Rally kept her shock to herself about the blush that skated up along the redhead's cheeks. Apparently, this woman made all the decisions and the three younger Jacksons didn't argue with her about it. She was the reigning monarch in this family.

She ate with them and thoroughly enjoyed the meal. After they cleaned, Grams went back to quilting while Rally picked up a book and read. She dozed off.

"You will be at the event, Zahra. Don't make me have to send guards to bring you there. I will not be pleasant." The king's tone held no warmth in it.

She glared up at the man who'd given her life. "I'm well aware of my role in this fiasco. I will be there and I will be the perfect princess that's required of me. Don't bother threatening me because it's never pleasant anyway."

His frown faltered for a moment, and for the briefest of seconds, she wondered if he would be the man she recalled growing up. Smiling, happy, proud of her. Then it vanished and she had her answer.

"You're a princess, it's time you acted like one instead of the spoiled brat you are."

"What role models do I have?" She tossed the question at him like a missile. "My siblings are worse than I am but you're pissed at me because I'm in the public eye, doing what I can to help the impoverished, the abused, those you don't give a damn about."

She spun on her heel and headed back to her room.

He didn't speak but she'd not expected him to. Her father hated being challenged yet some days she wondered if the man she used to call Daddy still remained beneath the royal mask he seemed cloaked in daily.

Behind her followed her bodyguards. Two tall, scowling men. She didn't like them, didn't trust them. But they were her father's men, so she accepted they reported back to him instead of being there for her. She didn't have friends, wasn't allowed.

She shut the door behind her and heaved a disappointed sigh. There went her plans for the night. Stepping into the marble bathroom, she turned on the shower as hot as she could handle it then stripped. When the temperature was right, she got beneath the streams and began prepping for the evening.

Her maid waited for her as she exited the shower and reached for a towel. "What are you doing in here?"

The young woman didn't meet her eyes, just kept her gaze on the floor. "I was sent by His Majesty. He said I should be helping you dress."

"I was going to call you after my shower. I know today is your birthday, Leah, and you were spending time with your family. I'm sorry you were pulled away." She wrapped the thick robe around her. "But I did get you something."

"No, princess. That's not necessary."

"Wrong. It's very necessary. You're the closest thing I have to a friend here and I wanted you to have something from me *on your birthday. Besides, like you said, I'm a princess, I can pretty much do what I want." Except get out of this damn event tonight.*

Leah trailed her into the main part of her room. More like a suite — she couldn't deny the opulence. She headed for her large vanity then opened a drawer with a small key and withdrew a box. Then she took it to her maid. "Here you go."

"Thank you, princess."

"Open it."

She carefully pulled the purple ribbon tied on the white box, then took off the lid. Rally waited as she lifted off the white cotton lying there to protect the gift.

"Oh, it's so beautiful." She shook her head. "I couldn't take this."

"It's yours. Has your name on it and everything."

Leah turned over the engraved nebula pendant attached to a gold chain. "To Leah. Happy 18th Birthday. Always look to the stars. From Princess Zahra." She looked at her, tears in her eyes.

"I wanted to make sure they knew it was a gift and not something you stole. I hope you like the nebula. I remembered how you were looking at the images in the store when I was getting books for the children. Thought this way you would have a piece of it with you at all times."

Leah's tears spilled over and Rally hugged her, ignoring the tensing as she did. It wasn't proper, but then she'd never been a proper princess. For her, this was what being rich was about, giving to those with less.

She handed Leah a tissue and gave her a gentle smile in the mirror as she fastened on her necklace. "Let's get me ready for this event."

Within twenty minutes, she was walking out of the room, flanked right away by the bodyguards, and heading to a place she didn't want to go. Her purple dress clung to her, showing off every curve. It was meant to entice. She felt like a piece of meat about to be sold to the highest bidder, which in essence she was.

Her blood chilled despite the heat of the day in Africa when her eyes landed on the man her father had told her would make a good match for him. That's right, for him, not her. He didn't care how it affected her, only himself and his kingdom.

It bothered her. While she spoke out for women's rights, this was occurring in her own land. It had happened to two of her sisters, and the fact one was in an abusive relationship didn't matter to her father either. It was kept behind closed doors. She'd discovered it by accident. When she told the king, he'd waved it off, stating her sister understood her duty.

A snarl turned up her lips ever so briefly. Her duty. A load of shit if she'd ever heard it. What about a father's duty to protect his children?

"Princess."

She blinked away memories and focused on the man bowing before her. Her 'good' match. He looked up at her, brown eyes watching her with an intensity that set her teeth on edge. Overly personal for him to be staring.

"Good evening, Mr. Frost."

His practiced grin added to her earlier unease. "We've known each other for a while. Call me Axel."

Rally woke with a start, heart pounding, and found she wasn't where she'd dozed off, but was instead inside Ethan's truck as it moved down the road. He hummed softly along with the music playing on the radio.

A blend of mortification and relief slammed into her and she struggled to sit up further. He angled his head toward her and gave her a smile in the dim lights from the dash.

"You're okay, princess."

"Don't call me that." Her words were edged and she shuddered. She liked Ethan a lot, and didn't want to associate past unpleasantness with that word and him. It didn't matter he'd called her this before. This most recent dream took away any possibility of her being okay with it continuing.

Chapter Ten

Ethan pulled the truck over to the side of the road and threw it into park. The anger in her tone surprised him. He'd gone over late in the evening to see how they were faring and found her crashed on a couch, his grandmother acting as if having a sleeping princess in her house was a common, everyday activity. He'd carried Rally out to the truck and berated himself for pushing her too hard.

But this anger at being called princess, he didn't understand. He faced her and turned on the dome light. Dark circles resided under her big eyes, her skin, still pale, worried him.

"What's going on, Rally?"

She shook her head and pulled into herself more. He sighed and reached for her, initiating the contact he believed they both needed. Holding her hand, he stroked the back of it.

"No hiding, Rally. Talk to me."

"Nothing to say." Her voice was so low he almost didn't pick up the words.

"Who called you princess?"

Her resigned sigh almost had him ashamed for pushing, but he wanted answers so it fell short.

"Axel Frost."

The man in the picture who watched her like he owned her. Or would be doing so soon. "And that's why you don't want me to call you that?"

Her chin wobbled then stopped. She lifted her head and he witnessed firsthand the transformation from regular person to royalty. "I would prefer being called Rally."

Perfect enunciation. No tone, no edge, but cold because he knew how Rally spoke. He had experienced her laughter, her moans. This was an ice cube of the woman he'd fallen for.

"Okay then, Rally. Come here."

She blinked, thrown by his comment. "What?"

He crooked his finger at her. "Come here."

"Why?"

"Unhook your belt and come here." He rested an arm on the back of the seat and waited.

She glanced around before obeying. Soon she sat in the middle, close to him. "Yes?"

"Thank you, I think I will."

Her brow furrowed. "I'm sorry, I'm not understanding."

He kissed her. Took her lips in his and slid his tongue in her waiting mouth. Her moan, bellows on the flames of his passion for her, making them explode to raging in seconds. Yes, she understood now. She mewled in the back of her throat before pressing closer to him. Still holding her hand, he drew back on it, bringing her arm

125

around his waist as he lifted her with his other hand under her ass so she sat on his lap.

Rally twined an arm around his neck and sank her fingers into his hair. God, he loved her touch. Nothing else could chase away the demons like she could. Their tongues dueled and danced with each other. Moans that had begun as separate melded into one.

He flexed his grip on her ass and she responded by grinding on his cock. He wanted her naked and surrounding his dick with her heat. "Rally," he muttered against her full lips.

"Ethan." Her throaty way of speaking his name was enough to put steel over his cock. She just didn't know the power she possessed.

She lifted her mouth from his and they stared at each other. He saw the windows and grinned. "Fogged them over. Guess we should get home and do this properly."

She didn't look away from him. "I agree."

He didn't release her and she wasn't in any rush to move away from him. Instead, she rocked against him, eliciting another groan from the depths of his throat.

"Rally," he rumbled. "Move now or I'm going to fuck you right here in my truck."

Her answer was to tighten her grip on his locks. Something left her mouth he couldn't interpret but he got the gist. He slipped a hand between them and freed himself as she shoved down her pants. It wasn't the prettiest, nor the easiest, but he didn't give a damn, and from the way her short, sharp breaths filled the air, neither did she.

He grunted in relief as he sank deep inside her wet heat. She enfolded him, welcomed him in her tight pussy. Ethan thrust up and she gasped as her head dropped back, offering her neck for him. He accepted the offer and nipped the side before licking away the sharp sting.

Grasping her breasts, he then plucked the taut nipples as she rode him. Her features, barely visible in the faint glow from his dash, still allowed him to see the passion on them. Lips parted, head back, eyes closed and moans sliding free were the best symphony he'd ever heard in his life.

She shivered as she came hard around his cock and he wasn't far behind her. Releasing her nipples, he gripped her hips, bringing her down hard to meet his upward thrusts. Once. Twice. And before he did it a third time, he moved one hand to cup the back of her neck and brought her close enough to kiss.

Lips light along hers, he flicked his tongue over them. "Regardless of what that fuck called you, Rally, you're mine. It doesn't matter if it's Rally, princess, or anything else. You. Are. *Mine*." He flexed his hold on her as he shot his seed deep inside her.

There wasn't any way he would be able to let this woman out of his life.

She didn't respond. At least not with verbal words, but she added her moans to his groans and grunts. All too soon she climbed off his lap and moved to the side where the steering wheel wasn't digging into her back.

It didn't take him long to put his softening cock back in his pants. Then he tugged her back to his side and wrapped an arm around her as he finished the drive back home. Rally didn't speak as they left his truck and moved up the steps to the door.

His home was warm and as he closed the night out, he took three seconds to glance at the security panel. Confident when it read 'secure,' he focused on the woman beside him. She continued to give off signs of a woman who'd been loved, thoroughly and proper.

She stood near the fireplace, one arm wrapped around her middle. He removed his boots and walked up behind her, bringing her into his embrace. Chin on her head, he stood there for a moment.

"What are you thinking?"

"How you'd be killed for what we just did."

That was a splash of cold-water reality. "Why are you thinking that?"

"Because we can't keep doing this. I don't want them to hurt you, Ethan. And I know that at some point I'll be going back home. I realize my time here with you is limited." She turned to face him. "I care too much for you to take this risk."

"You were with Rolf for three years. I was there for one. I don't give a monkey's fuck about the protocol that your family deems proper. *We* have a bond — we share something, something they won't ever understand. If we want to fuck like bunnies, then we will. Nothing will change that."

Her eyes blanked and that emotionless look owned her face. Ethan didn't understand. Had he said something wrong? Couldn't be. Surely she got what he was trying to say.

"You're right." The words may have been correct, however the tone was as off as a purple elephant walking down Peachtree in Atlanta. "I'm really tired. If you'll excuse me." She ducked away from his touch and moved down the stairs to what he presumed to be her bedroom.

"What the fuck just happened?"

Fifteen minutes later, after his shower, dressing, checking on Rally — who was out cold — he stood in his computer room, had images on all the screens as he attempted to figure out who the fuck this Axel Frost was in his real-life persona. The image was running through all databases, including Interpol, CIA, NSA and a few that people still didn't know about.

He leaned back in his chair and groaned, running his hands over his eyes. The smell of coffee had him jerking upright. Beau strode into the room, two mugs in hand, and silently offered him one. Behind him walked Anabelle Lee, a drink of her own in hand.

"What are y'all two doing here?"

"Not just us. Mino and Masters are still getting their drinks." Beau sat his large body down on the couch and stretched out his legs.

He sighed. "Fine, what are all y'all doing here?"

"Came to see how things were going with you and if there wasn't anything we could help with." Masters spoke as he strode in, his perpetual scowl in place. Behind him came Mino whose upbeat attitude more than offset Masters' cranky one.

Mino glanced at him. "How are you doing?"

Was better when I had my dick sank deep inside Rally. "I'm coping. Still having nightmares, but getting through them."

"And Rally?" Mino moved close to him, ignoring the way Beau had his big feet stretched out in the way. She kicked him and glared until he moved them. "How are her nightmares?"

"She doesn't talk about them much. I've tried but she clams up." Another point that irked the hell out of him. Why wouldn't she share them with him?

"Any more memory return?"

"This man, Axel Frost, is worrying her. On some level I think even more than Rolf." He glanced over to another screen where the rendition of Rolf also ran through the databases. Still no hit there. "I can't tell her anything about him and she's not exactly forthcoming with all she knows. She's hiding something but I'm not sure why." He drank his coffee, burning his mouth, and rose to get some more. Mino followed him.

"What else is it?" she asked as he poured himself a refill.

"Nothing."

"Don't bullshit a bullshitter. Something else is bothering you about Rally." She moved to his side but didn't touch him like Anabelle Lee would. Mino didn't do a lot of touching.

"I told her that her family could go fuck themselves because we had been through something they'd never understand. And if we wanted to fuck each other we could, to hell with the ramifications."

She stirred the spoon in her porcelain mug. "Please tell me you didn't say it that way."

"Close."

"And she's shut down?"

"Yes." He added a liberal dose of sugar.

"And you're not understanding why." Mino clucked her tongue. "Men. You basically told her that because you were both there, it was okay to fuck. Nothing about feelings. She's a princess, Ethan. She's already going to be berated and screamed at for no longer being a virgin. But she's given herself to you and you say it's okay because of both being a prisoner? That's got nothing to do with feelings for her. My guess, you just broke her heart."

Beau walked in and looked between the two of them. "What took you so long to get here, Mino? Masters said you weren't coming with him."

"Not that my life is your concern, Beauregard, but I was on a date."

He ran blue eyes over her. "Not dressed up but that looks more like PJs."

"We were at that point of the date." She sneered at him before giving Ethan a small smile. "Fix that." Then she headed out of the room.

Shit. If that was how Rally saw it, he had a lot of work to do. Beau topped off his coffee and waited to walk to the other room with him.

* * * *

Rally stood at the railing, overlooking the melting snow. Apparently, this was how the weather should be around here. Cold but the snow almost vanished. Her nights were full of Ethan or nightmares. As if he knew, he never missed the opportunity to hold her as the sun sank.

Right now, he was inside with Masters as they went over information she had given. More on the first place she'd been kept. It wasn't much but it was all she'd been able to give them. Even so, she wasn't confident it wasn't just her imagination that had created something as her mind scrambled to make sense of what she'd been through.

He'd filled out, showing her the strong man he had been born to be. Whenever they were in a room together, she couldn't take her eyes off him. He had become her addiction.

She'd put on some much-needed weight as well and tried her damnedest to hide her nightmares. Ethan always knew. More often than not, he pushed to get her to open up.

"What are you doing out here?"

Rally glanced over her shoulder to where Mino approached with a smile on her face.

"Thinking." She brushed her gloved hand over the railing before gripping the smooth wood. "What about you?"

"Came to check on you. Masters and Ethan are still talking." She angled so she faced Rally. "Are you okay?" One hand moved through the air. "I mean, I know that's a shitty question to ask, especially given what you've been through, but I'm worried you are still having nightmares and don't look as if you're getting much sleep. Is there anything I can get for you?"

Unlike when someone offered something similar that to her back home, with Mino, she believed there were nothing more than her best interests at heart. Not an angle to get a favor later on down the road from a princess.

She mulled over her words before speaking them. "I feel it is time for me to return home. We both must get on with our lives."

"Ethan's not going to want to let you go."

Well, she didn't wish to leave so there you were. Instead of voicing that, she shrugged. "He should be back to work. He's pushing to go out there with his sister and cousin. I am holding him back."

"Oh, honey, please don't think that. You're not holding him back. Ethan will go return when he's ready and not a minute sooner. These Jackson people are a stubborn lot."

"And I have responsibilities to attend to myself." Her heart ached at the thought of leaving Ethan.

"I'll tell you they're worried about this Axel Frost. Not to mention Rolf."

"I'll be protected."

Mino arched an eyebrow. "You had them around you the first time."

She had. "True but I was also in an airplane. It will be different in the palace."

"He won't let you leave until he's sure you will be safe. Even then I'm not positive he will agree to you returning to your country."

"You know them well, yes?"

"I've worked with all of them for a good number of years now." She faced the property, arms resting on the rail. "Why?"

"Then you know how dedicated they are to their cause. I am a distraction he can't afford to have. They're trying to find out who this person is bringing down the planes, who the man named Rolf is plus whatever else they do."

"Keeping you safe is on that list as well. I'm telling you, Rally, Ethan's not going to go for it."

"Go for what?"

Rally shared a look with Mino at the interrupting question. It was Anabelle Lee.

"Me leaving," Rally said.

The redhead raked her cold gaze over her before crossing her arms. "You're leaving?"

"I think it's time."

"I agree."

"Christ, Anabelle Lee," Mino muttered. "Can't even pretend to be nice?"

"I don't do nice." She never pulled her gaze from Rally even though she spoke to Mino. "When are you heading out?"

She didn't understand why this woman didn't like her but it wasn't the first time she'd encountered hatred

and she doubted it would be the last. "As soon as I can."
*No point in hanging around here to get more attached to the
man I've already fallen for.*

"Mino's right. He's not going to like it, nor let you go.
I'll take you. I'll make the reservations and take you
where you need to go."

Mino crossed her arms and glared at Anabelle Lee.
"She doesn't have to go anywhere."

"I'm helping her get home." Blue eyes cut to Mino
then back to Rally. "I'll purchase your ticket and pick
you up tomorrow. Tell Ethan I'm taking you to Grams'
again. He'll believe that."

"What a fucking bitch," Mino groused before
gripping her arm. "You don't have to go anywhere,
Rally."

"Mino!" Masters' bellow shoved in the conversation.

"What?" she cried back.

"Need you inside." He shut the door and Mino
mumbled about his bossiness as she headed to the
warmth.

"You don't have to go, Rally. No matter what some
people say." Then she was gone.

Alone with Anabelle Lee, Rally maintained her
expressionless features. The woman may scare the shit
out of her but she refused to show her the truth about
that. Instead, she lifted her chin and held the gaze that
had no warmth in its depths.

"What's it going to be?"

"I have a choice?" Rally asked, an edge to her own
tone.

"Of course. I'm not going to kidnap you and take you
away. But I think you should get home to your family.
There can't be anything between you and my brother.
We both know that won't be allowed, and the longer

you stay around him, the more he is going to fall. Which will end up with you hurting him more and me wanting to kill you."

She stated it as if she were saying how she preferred to eat a grapefruit versus an apple.

"Were we in my country, you would be killed for such a statement." Haughtiness tinged her words.

Anabelle Lee barely blinked. "One, we're not, and two, they could try."

"Is it just me you have an issue with or is it anyone who may turn your brother's head?"

"I'll back off when it's the right woman."

Nausea churned her gut at the thought of another with Ethan, experiencing his touch skimming along their body. The way he brought her to a fevered pitch. His kisses. The glide of his thick cock as it pushed into her, how he could thrust and make her toes curl, make her scream until her throat was raw, or make love to her tender enough to make her cry.

"And that's not me."

"Nope. He needs a woman who can live like this. Not a princess."

I did ask. She didn't divulge how much she loved being here, away from the palace that never gave her a moment's peace. "I'll be ready tomorrow." She walked away, head high, trying to wrap her thoughts around the fact this was her last night with him. Tears burned but she blinked them away then she stepped inside.

Ethan appeared before she could make it down the stairs. He moved to her side and brushed a kiss along her temple. "You're cold. What were you doing outside?"

"Talking to Mino and Anabelle Lee."

"Glad you're getting along with both of them."

Fifty percent wasn't bad. Was it? She smiled up at him and patted his hand before heading down to the room. Ethan hadn't moved her into his room, allowing her to keep her own. Not that she slept alone but the option was there at least.

She paused in the doorway and gazed about, taking in the simple furniture, the view from the window that overlooked his beautiful property and the color scheme. All of it meshed together perfectly.

More so when she compared it to her room in the palace. The gold-gilded bed. Lace and velvets. Heavily perfumed curtains and furniture. Hell, half the time she was afraid of what may happen if she broke it. She could sell one item and feed people for a long time. She had been doing that for a while until her father had put a stop to her actions.

Rebel or not, she obeyed the king. Doing things on a smaller scale. Perhaps doing more charity work would help her figure out how to get back on track with her life.

Damn it, I'm going to miss him.

"Ready for dinner?"

She turned to face the man who lounged in the doorway. He filled out his jeans in a way that made her wet. When he reached his full strength, he was going to be bloody amazing. His gray shirt hugged his broad shoulders and hung down, hiding his defined abs. *How unfortunate.* She could stare at him forever. Yes, she would miss him.

Pushing to her feet, she nodded as she approached. Ethan Jackson wasn't a man she would ever forget.

Chapter Eleven

"Thanks for helping me out, Anabelle Lee. I know Grams enjoyed spending time with her. I've got some therapy to go to."

His sister gave him a smile. "Masters actually got you to go?"

"Not willingly but I woke up last night and had a gun in my hand before I knew what was going on. I can't be that jumpy. I may injure myself or someone else. He won't put me back in the field if I can't handle sleep."

She nodded, her thick red hair braided and in a single rope over her left shoulder, breaking through the stark white of her jacket. "I understand. You know I'm here if you want to talk."

"I know you are and I thank you so much for being the best sister in the world, but this isn't anything you can help with. I have to come to terms with it on my own." More facts that bothered the fuck out of him.

"I'll be to your place in about fifteen minutes, just tell her to be ready."

Part of what made Anabelle Lee so damn good at what she did was her ability to separate it all, yet the fact she didn't make any further comment on his not being able to talk to her rang wrong in his ear. He would have to ask her about that later when he had some free time.

"Will do." He ended the call with his sister. Shoving the phone in his pocket, he called out, "Rally?"

"Downstairs."

He smiled and jogged down to find her in the bedroom he'd first put her in, drawing her hair up into a ponytail.

"Anabelle Lee is on her way. She said she'd be here in about fifteen minutes."

"Fine."

He narrowed his eyes slightly. Rally wouldn't meet his gaze.

"What's going on?"

Now she did. Eyebrows up, she shook her head as she pulled slightly on her hair to make sure it was secure. "I'm not sure I understand."

Ethan approached her and slipped his arms around her waist. "I think you do. Something is going on. What is it?"

"I'm just nervous. I don't want to do or say anything that will offend your grandmother."

He understood this — many people were intimidated by Grams. She was a tempest and her own force to be reckoned with. "She loved you the first time and she will again."

"I don't quite have the confidence you do."

"Sure you do," he muttered in her ear, swiping his tongue along the whorl. "You just don't want to show it to people. You like being in the background, being overlooked. Unless you're at one of your causes speaking out."

Her entire body sank into his.

"That's true. I miss those events but I will be back to them one day."

Ethan didn't mind. He loved her passion witnessed in those videos he'd seen of her, fighting her good fight. It was the only time he'd seen her in the news. Her siblings were there often for being at clubs, run-ins with the law, and other things. But not her. She was persona non grata until there was a cause she believed in. Then there she stood front and center, using her platform to bring recognition to the problem.

"You will." Even as the words left his lips, he had doubts on if he wanted that to happen. What were the choices for a princess and a man embroiled in the world of espionage?

Anabelle Lee had been correct on a few things – theirs wasn't a match made in heaven. Ethan hadn't gotten to the place to willingly let her leave his life. If she had no wish to tell her family she was alive, he had no problems with that fact. He wanted her to stay with him.

He began swaying back and forth, with her still in his arms. Her gaze held his.

"What are you doing?"

"Is it weird that when I have you in my arms I hear music?"

There it was. Her smile. Brilliant and jumper cables to his heart. She didn't share large smiles like that often but his heart tripped over itself the few times she had.

"I think you are still crazy."

He kissed her cheek. "No argument here. Have fun today, okay?"

"I will do my best." Rally turned in his arms and looped hers about his neck. "Thank you, Ethan. For everything. For not leaving me in that hellhole and for not killing me when I was sure you wanted to."

He began to shake his head. She placed a hand over his mouth.

"I require nothing from you, I only wanted to say thank you."

He nipped at her palm and kissed her when she moved her hand away. "You aren't like any princess I know."

Her brown eyes were warm, welcoming him in like vats of melted chocolate. "And you are acquainted with a lot of them?"

"I don't believe I have ever met a single one aside from you," he lied. He'd met several doing his job but they weren't important to him.

"Well then, how would you know?"

"Fine, allow me to correct myself. I believe you are different than how they are portrayed to be."

"I would agree with that assessment. Now, enough of this. I have to go, you have to go. We both have appointments and can't afford to be late."

"You and I are having a date night tonight." Another kiss and he set her away from him before he said to hell with their plans and took her to bed.

She gave him a shy smile. "Have a good day, Ethan."

"You too, Rally." One more kiss then he jogged outside to where Beauregard and Mino waited.

He nodded at his cousin and placed a kiss on Mino's cheek. She blinked at him a few times then smiled as tears filled her eyes.

"What did I do now?"

She hugged him. "Nothing new, just you used to kiss my cheek each time you saw me. This was the first time since you were rescued."

"Guess I'm settling in then." While he knew that wasn't completely true, it was something Mino needed to hear. Her smile broadened and she hugged him once more.

"What about me?"

Beauregard's question broke the heaviness of the moment, even more so when Mino glared at him and flipped him the bird.

"If it's all the same to you, Beauregard," she said, tone dripping with more fake sweetener than anything had a right to be doused in. "I'd just as soon keep myself creature free."

His smile, known to charm the panties off all women, appeared as he winked. "Are you sure about that, darlin'? I've been told I'm an animal in bed."

Ethan rolled his eyes.

Mino didn't back away for a second. She gave Beauregard a 'bless your heart' smile. "I've heard that too, and you must be proud, but I'm not really one for crabs or other small infestational creatures. Thanks anyway." She walked away and climbed into the large truck idling in his driveway.

"You can't help it, can you?" Ethan asked Beauregard.

"It's all part of my charm."

"Yes, I can see how well that's working out for you."

"I'm wearing her down."

He laughed. "No you're not. You're going to end up bleeding because you've pushed her too far."

"Mino knows I'm only joking with her."

Ethan wasn't so sure. "Let's get this over with."

Two steps down and he paused when Beauregard clapped him on the shoulder. Ethan hated the fear that fizzled through him at something as simple as a touch from his cousin. He kept it off his face and glanced back.

"Yes?"

"I get we don't talk about our feelings but you know I'm here if you need me, right? We don't have to talk. We can just sit up at night if you're having difficulty sleeping."

"Thanks. I do. You're always there if I need you. Both of you. I thought I'd be better by now but the nightmares won't stop and neither does my mind-numbing fear. So if it takes me seeing this damn shrink to get by it, then so be it."

"And your princess?"

"She could teach us a thing or two about not sharing anything. Even her nightmares are contained before I can ask her about them. She's like a wall, refusing to give me anything."

"It's bothering you."

"Damn straight it is. I know what shit I went through. She's a woman and a princess, I'm sure she hadn't ever figured on having to go through what she did."

"Neither did you."

They hit the ground and headed for his cousin's truck.

"I know but I've had training for what I endured. She hasn't."

Beauregard just grunted and opened the driver's door of his jacked-up Dodge and hopped in. Ethan climbed up on the passenger side. Mino sat behind them, eyes on the tablet in her hand.

"Miss me?" Beau teased her.

"Like always," she retorted with a bland tone.

"See, cuz, I'm the star of one woman's fantasies."

Ethan angled his head to look at the woman in the back seat. She didn't even look up at him, just ignored him and his cousin.

"Sure you are," he said. "Mino missed you so much she's unable to tear herself from the tablet in hand."

"A ruse, man, it's all a ruse. She secretly wants me."

"So secret you're the only one who knows."

Another smile flashed and Beau laughed. "Exactly, which means I'm halfway there. I only have to convince one more person."

Ethan joined in but Mino was absent of entering the joviality. With another peek back to her, he noticed the frown on her face as she scrolled through the stuff on her screen.

He wanted to ask her a question but she took a call from Masters, so he faced front and tried to convince himself that getting to this shrink would be for the best.

* * * *

"Are you ready?"

Rally turned to find the striking redhead standing in the doorway to her room. Correction, to her temporary room. Her insides screamed their refusal.

She stood, lifted her chin, and said, "Of course."

Anabelle Lee gestured to the small bag she'd packed earlier. "Is that all you're taking?"

"I have one change of clothes and toiletries. Is this not acceptable to you?" She didn't bother hiding the condemnation in her tone.

Ethan's sister arched her finely sculpted brow. "I assumed you would take everything he got for you."

"That's your issue, not mine."

She walked by her, out of the door and upstairs to the kitchen where she grabbed a quick glass of water. Her heart broke. She loved it here, loved being with Ethan and, no matter how little she liked Anabelle Lee, she couldn't fault her for protecting her brother.

The woman didn't make a sound, just wasn't there, then was a second later. After rinsing out the glass and setting it in the dishwasher, she picked up the small bag and faced the door. "Let's go then."

Nothing was spoken between them as they went to Anabelle Lee's truck. It was like Ethan's and Beauregard's, except white. Same jacked-up height with the big grill and winch on the front.

Rally sighed as she pulled herself up to the passenger seat and buckled her belt. Bag secure between her feet, she waited for her driver.

My driver, oh she'd probably hate being called that. I'll have one again soon enough.

Struggling, Rally dug for some confidence to make it through the upcoming ordeal. Anabelle Lee hopped up and started the powerful engine.

"I have your passport waiting and I did alert your family, so I believe they will have someone, or a few someones, at the airport for you." She cleared her throat. "They wanted to pick you up where you were but I said you'd meet them at the airport, that the people who'd saved you wanted to remain anonymous."

"Thank you for protecting Ethan."

"I'm his sister. It's what I was born to do. He's family."

Another jab on how Rally wasn't. She let it go. Arguing with Anabelle Lee accomplished nothing at all.

"Won't they be able to trace your vehicle?"

"We're just going to see Masters. He has one for us that's linked to a rental company and when they dig it will be shown as some faceless corporation. The driver won't know anything either. They were just paid to take you to the destination."

She understood. Even so, it irked her that Anabelle Lee couldn't even be bothered to take her to the airport herself but had pawned her off on someone else. Sure, it made sense why she was doing it, but that didn't stop the irritation.

They stopped at a small pulloff and Anabelle Lee killed the motor then jumped out. Rally followed at a slower pace. Masters stood beside the black town car with its tinted windows, arms crossed over his massive chest.

"You know Ethan is going to be pissed with you for this," he commented to the redhead.

"He'll get over it once he realizes this was the best thing for him." Anabelle Lee tucked some hair behind her ear.

Rally narrowed her gaze. *That's the first feminine thing I've ever seen her do. Why isn't she being her normal combative self with this man?*

"Are you ready, Rally?" Masters called to her.

His question derailed her thoughts and clenching her fingers about the strap of the bag she carried, she nodded. "I am."

Not in any way even remotely ready for this.

He held the door for her and she slid into the darkened interior. There was a divider up so she couldn't even see the driver. Masters leaned in the back.

"I wish things could have been different for the two of you."

Rally spied Anabelle Lee hovering near and listening in. "Like Ms. Jackson was fond of pointing out, I'm a princess and the Jackson family is *far* from royalty." She tossed her head. "Thank you for bringing me home."

"If you have any more leads," he began.

"I'll have our lawyers contact you. Goodbye, Mr. Masters." She dismissed him as if she were at home and waited for him to close the door.

"Damn, I'm going to miss you." She barely heard him mutter those words as he shut the door and pounded on the roof.

The car drew away and she settled back, getting herself ready for whatever lay around the next corner. There was no more room for Ethan in her thoughts — she was about to be shoved back into the vipers' nest and she had to be sharp or she'd end up dead before she made it back to Africa.

When the car stopped, she peered out of the window. It was a small airport, executive. The kind she used to fly into. Peering a bit more left, she saw a familiar sight, a Dassault Falcon 2000EX.

Interesting. It's not what my family flies. It's what Axel came to see us with. Her breathing slowed as she thought of having to cross the ocean with that man as her only traveling companion.

The door opened and she took a deep breath before stepping out. The driver relieved her of the bag and carried it to the jet. Two figures exited the jet and hurried down to the tarmac.

She didn't recognize them.

"Welcome home, princess."

She ran a critical gaze over them. "And who are you?"

"They're my men, princess."

That was a voice she recognized. Axel Frost.

She peered up to see him approaching them. She inclined her head. "Mr. Frost."

His smile sent shivers up her spine as he neared her.

"We've known each other longer than the need for formality." He opened his arms as if to hug her.

She flinched and held up a hand. "I'm sorry," she said, adding a wobble to her voice. "I'm still jumpy."

Her words appeased him and he nodded. "Of course, how insensitive of me to forget the trials you went through. I know you were hoping to see your family but I was in the States and offered to bring you back." He glanced over his shoulder. "Let's get you on board."

With Axel beside her and the bodyguards flanking them, she ascended the stairs. Each one she climbed, the shell around her snapped into place. Though still damaged, she was fortified by her refusal to give in to the horrors she'd suffered, or to allow anyone to use her like that again.

He gestured her to a seat then took one opposite her. A flight attendant brought him a drink and left with a smile as well as a smack on the ass.

At one time Rally would have been outraged, but right now, she wasn't about to make any waves, she needed to get home. After she got settled in there, she could see to things like that.

"Would you care to sleep or are you up for talking about what happened?"

"Sleep would be wonderful."

She noted the frustration in his expression but he didn't push her, just nodded. "Of course. Once we're up in the air feel free to use my cabin and sleep as much as you need."

"Thank you, Mr. Frost."

"Axel, please, Zahra. Again, we know each other well enough." A smile that curdled her stomach lifted his lips. "And hopefully we will be able to know each other better still."

She didn't answer, just looked out of the window as Georgia grew smaller and smaller with each minute of the Falcon rising into the skies. That portion of her life was over — she couldn't afford to think about her lover any longer. Ethan had his life to live and Rally had hers to survive.

Chapter Twelve

"Ethan, you'd better come look at this!"

Beauregard's shout snapped him from the work he was trying to accomplish on the computer his cousin had asked him to fix.

"What?" he called back. "I'm a bit busy here, fixing this clusterfuck you did. How you did this to your computer I'm still not sure."

"Get the hell out here, now!"

It wasn't normal for Beau to sound that way so he dropped the items in his hand and hurried out to his cousin's living room. They'd come here after his therapy to relax and apparently fix this computer that was giving him issues.

"What the hell, man?"

Beau had his hat off and ran a hand through his hair as he pointed at the television screen.

Ethan glanced at it and in the next second had to reach for support as his legs gave out. On the screen was a picture of Rally, dressed to the nines as a princess should be. The rose dress she wore did amazing things to her body.

Below the image was the caption—*Presumed dead princess on her way back home.*

"What the fuck?" he gasped.

"I don't know. Anabelle Lee isn't answering and neither is Rally. I'm trying Masters now."

"Turn the sound up," he ordered.

Beau listened and they paid attention to the reporter.

"It was a great shock to the royal house to learn that the youngest daughter Zahra, who'd been presumed dead for years when her plane went down over the Coral Sea, was coming home. This news is still coming in and we'll update as soon as we know more, but right now, all we can tell you is she's on a jet flying from somewhere in Georgia back to Africa. We've not been able to get a location on where she left from or who she was staying with all this time while her family mourned her."

A sheet of paper was slipped in front of the news anchor.

"One moment please, I just received this. It appears that she was held captive for those years and managed to escape. No mention of how she escaped or who assisted her. Just that she contacted her family and they sent a trusted friend to bring her back. A Mr. Axel Frost."

His breath left him and his head swam with all this news. *What the fuck happened?*

Digging for his phone, he immediately tried Rally, but as Beau said, there wasn't any answer, it went to voicemail. The commentator continued but the words didn't make any sense. He tried Rally once more and left a message.

"Rally, call me the second you get this." Then he dialed his sister. "Anabelle Lee, where the fuck are you? Call me! Why am I seeing that Rally is on her way home with none other than Axel Frost?"

He swore repeatedly as he tossed down his phone then tuned back in to the news.

"We will have reports live when she lands in a few hours and hopefully the spokesperson for the royal family will be available to make a statement. Stay tuned for more details as we'll share them with you as we receive them."

They cut to commercial and he rubbed his chest. This wasn't good. Not at all.

Beauregard met his gaze and shook his head. "Nothing from Masters either."

Ethan reached for his phone once more and dialed another number.

"What's up, Ethan?"

His heart surged with emotion. "Mino. Where's Masters?"

"Not sure. Haven't seen him since this morning. He headed out to take care of a few things but he's not been back yet. His schedule is clear. Did you want me to have him call you?"

"Yes dammit, as soon as possible. Beau and I are watching the news report that Rally is on her way home. I'm trying to figure out how that happened."

"She did it, damn it."

He frowned and snapped his fingers to his cousin. "She who did what?"

Mino was quiet for a moment.

"Tell me what you're talking about, Mino?" He put her on speakerphone. "Who is the she and what did she do?"

"This is not my place to get into or my business. I suggest you speak to your sister on this, Ethan. I'll get in touch with Masters."

"I've tried his phone and he's not answering. And what do you mean? What does Anabelle Lee have to do with any of this?"

"Talk to your sister. I'm refusing to get in this and Masters has another phone he always has on him. I'll tell him to give you a call." She ended their conversation before he could say another word.

"What the fuck is going on around here? Did you know about his other phone?"

"No clue about it." Beau muted the television.

Ethan paced then stomped his way back to the room he had been working in and sat before the computer, his mind whirling with possibilities. All of them unpleasant.

Thankfully, computer repair was mindless work for him and he got to it. When his phone rang later, he lunged for it.

"Rally?"

"No. Mino said you wanted to speak to me."

"Where's my Rally?"

His boss didn't speak for a moment and Ethan, who hung on to the last vestiges of his patience, waited.

"I suspect you know the answer to that question. I've no doubt you have seen the news."

"What did you do?" Anger roiled below the surface and he struggled to retain the slightest bit of control.

Beside him, Beau cocked an eyebrow in his direction and he waved his cousin off. One thing at a time.

"I did as she requested."

"She who?"

"Princess Zahra."

"Bullshit," he spat. "You'll never convince me she wanted to go home. She could have requested that since the moment she got here and never once did she say she wanted to get back to the palace. In fact, her actions speak to the complete opposite of that, so I'll ask you once more. What the fuck did you do?"

"I already answered that. I did as she requested."

Ethan stood, hand fisted at his side. "You need to name the time and place where we can meet and discuss this."

"Don't assume because I'm the boss means I can't hold my own or kick your ass, Ethan. You bring this on, I'm not going to hold back because you're not one hundred percent."

He narrowed his gaze. "I'm more than capable of holding my own against you, Masters. You've never wanted her here except to answer your damn questions. Name the time and place."

"I'll be by your house this evening."

"See you don't forget." He ended the call and swore another litany that would have had his grandmother tanning his ass with a switch.

"You seriously going to tangle with Masters?"

"The fucker sent her home. He will pay for that."

Beauregard crossed his arms over his tattered green John Deere shirt and cracked his neck. "I hate to mention this—"

"Then don't."

"But," he continued, unperturbed by Ethan's snappish outburst, "wasn't she supposed to be with Anabelle Lee this morning at Grams'?"

It bothered him to think his sister accepted a part in this subterfuge. With Masters he could see it, the man played by his own set of rules. But Anabelle Lee was blood.

"I'm going to see Grams."

Beauregard swiped his hat and followed him out. "I'm not missing this for anything."

The ride to his grandmother's was fast and tense. He drummed his fingers along his thigh. Even so, he slowed to what his grams thought to be an acceptable speed on her driveway and parked before the house.

She sat on the porch, despite the cold weather, and worked on a quilt.

Her smile never failed to make him grateful for her being in his life. He hopped up on the porch and pressed a kiss to her cheek. "Hey, Grams."

She turned her cheek to accept a kiss from Beau then shuffled her gaze between the two of them. "What's wrong?"

Beau held up his hands and stepped back. "I'm along for the ride."

Grams narrowed her eyes at him but never stopped quilting. "Ethan?" she asked, setting down the section in her hand and digging for another fat quarter to attach. "I'm not getting any younger."

"I thought Anabelle Lee and Rally were supposed to be here with you?"

"Anabelle Lee is on her way, said she was stopping to pick up some more paints to take home with her first. She never mentioned Rally." She frowned. "Did you lose her?"

"In a manner of speaking, yes."

His Grams shot her head up and speared him with blue eyes that were like his own.

"Meaning what exactly? That girl is still recovering from the trauma she went through and doesn't need to be exposed to any more."

"I know that, Grams. But I was told that she was going to be over here with you today."

"Heavens no. I've not seen her at all today. Why would Anabelle Lee lie about that?"

Her white truck turned up the driveway and Ethan experienced a flash of anger toward his sister. "We're about to find out."

He met her as she climbed down from her Dodge.

"What the fuck did you do?" he demanded, fists at his sides.

"Hello to you too, brother."

He raked his gaze over her. Red hair up in a ponytail, jeans and a black leather jacket. Blue eyes that didn't back down from his challenge.

"I'm not in the mood, Anabelle Lee. Tell me why you did it?"

"I did it for you. She's not the right woman for you, and the longer you allowed her to stick around, the less you were realizing that fact."

"At least you're not denying it."

"Why would I? And let Masters alone. He helped because I asked him to. This is on me, not anyone else. Well, me and your princess."

The sneer encompassing her tone when the word princess fell from her lips yanked a growl from his throat. He lunged at her, pushing her back into the truck.

"Ethan! Unhand your sister right this instant. I didn't raise you to act like that. You have a problem, you talk about it."

He released her instantly and turned to look at his grandmother. "Sorry, Grams, she went too far this time, I have nothing to say to her. And if Rally is killed back at her home because of this, I'll never have anything to say to her again." He sliced his gaze back to his sister. "You went too fucking far this time. Stay away from me and out of my way."

Hurt flashed in her gaze before she hid it from him. "It was for your own good," she reiterated.

"You don't know what is for my own good. You're being a selfish bitch, wanting her out of the way because I brought her home with me." He stepped closer to Anabelle Lee. "I didn't mind you interfering when the women were useless bitches but Rally was different. I'm in love with her. All you did to satisfy your childish feelings was to put her in more danger. I hope you're proud of yourself."

He spun on his heel and got back in his truck, this time leaving with a flurry of spinning tires and gravel. Metal blaring in his ears as he drove, he headed home but continued past until he got to a park he'd not been to in years. He jumped out and stalked along a path, ignoring the cold biting at his exposed skin.

"You know, if you're going to be out here, you should at least dress for the occasion."

"Fuck off, Masters, I'm not in the mood."

"You're the one who wanted to see me."

Ethan turned in time to catch the heavy jacket his boss lobbed at him. Shoving his arms into it, he couldn't help the grunt at the warmth that covered him.

Masters watched him with expressionless black eyes. "Here I am."

"You helped my sister send her home where she has no protection."

"I doubt that. She's probably well protected."

"By the people who let her get taken in the first place?" he snarled. "I fail to see how that's helpful to her."

Masters sighed and adjusted the fingers on his black gloves. "We can't save everyone, Ethan."

"I know that and I don't give a fuck you didn't come after me. It's what I signed up for. But she didn't."

"Zahra is stronger than you think."

"Her name is *Rally*," he bit off.

"That's a nickname and one you shouldn't be using anymore. She's gone, Ethan. Face it. You are not in the position to be calling her such a familiar name. People will be coming around and asking questions about who knew there was a lost princess in Georgia, and, while my sources are better than most, there's still a chance she will be linked to you. If and when that happens, you need to be Ethan Jackson, computer tech guru and not the man who fancies himself in love with a princess, taking offense at what others say and appearing as if he will kill anyone who threatens her."

"I hate you."

"I can live with that." There was no remorse in Masters' voice.

"Is this how you were with Lexy?"

"No. But she's a veterinarian, not a princess." He faced him. "And look what happened when news got out about her being involved with Valentino. Can you imagine what that would be like for a princess? Not only your enemies would be after her but also her family's enemies."

"Just have it all worked out then, don't you, Masters? Is everything so damn black and white in your world?"

"Yes. I don't have the luxury of seeing it any other way. I have a country depending on me to keep on top of it all. Hell, a world."

He crossed his arms. "And what do you do when you hang your cape up at night then, Superman?"

"Haven't you figured it out yet? I don't hang it up."

"I can't wait for you to fall in love. Then tell me this is all for the best."

"Love isn't a luxury I'm allowed to have."

"I'd feel sorry for you but you brought that on yourself. As much of an ass as you are, there's someone out there for you." He faced the way they came. "I need some time. Don't contact me unless absolutely necessary." Ethan strode off without a look back or another word.

Back at his house, he went to the room that, until today, had been Rally's. He could still pick up on her faint scent. He missed her already. Opening the closet, he stared at the clothing she didn't pack. *Mino can take it somewhere and give it to someone who needs it.* There wasn't anything left of her in there. The bathroom had been cleaned out. The bed made, it was as if she'd not been there to begin with.

Heart hurting, he lay on the bed, same side as she had used. The pillow also retained a hint of her shampoo. Which technically was his but somehow it had smelled so much better on her than him.

Lying there, he stared at the bedside table and frowned, adjusting a bit more to see toward the back where a piece of paper had been taped. After pulling it free, he lay on his back and opened it.

The sheet had her neat script on it and he read what she'd put.

~Water that's not water – fake, something below the surface.

~man with Axel Frost, Carlos something. Looks similar to a man I saw in a picture with Anabelle Lee.

~their motto: Oderint dom netuant, Latin like the words written on Ethan's side. Completely different meanings. Continue to trust Ethan and hope I can remember more about the other group for him and Masters.

~tell Ethan I've fallen in love with him? No, too risky. Plus, his sister would never approve. Not bringing trouble between them.

He gulped and had to steady his hand. She loved him. More an issue with his sister but he could focus on that later. Right now, he had to think about that other Latin phrase.

Unlike Beauregard, he didn't speak Latin. He took his stairs a few at a time and typed it in his computer, searching for a translation.

"Let them hurt so long as they fear," he read from the screen.

Holy shit. He'd seen that before. Sending it to Mino, he sat down and began poring through his notes to find where and when he'd come across that motto.

* * * *

"What can you tell me about the people who helped you?"

Rally glanced up from the book she was attempting to read during the last leg of the flight to the palace.

"If it's all the same to you, Mr. Frost, I would like to tell the story once. Not a multitude of times." She put her attention back on the mystery she'd found stashed in his bedroom. Not her typical read, but she was willing to read anything to keep from having to speak to this man.

"So you've said for the entire trip."

"Yet you keep inquiring." She closed the book, marking her page with one finger. "Is there a reason for that, aside from your lack of respect for my wishes?" She pitched her voice low so the bodyguards wouldn't be able to overhear their exchange.

He narrowed his eyes. "You have a lot of sass for someone who's been missing for years."

She arched an eyebrow and stared down her nose at him, as if she were at home, in her palace. "No, I don't. I'm a princess, and, regardless of your relationship with my family, I expect to be treated as such. Were we at the palace, your questions would be unacceptable, and they are here as well."

"I offered a favor."

She leaned closer. "For which we both know you are expecting some kind of reward since you never do anything for the pure goodness of your heart." She sat back. "I am not answering your questions before I speak with the king. You can be as frustrated and upset about that as you like. It won't change a thing. Then once the official statement has been given, you'll know, as will the rest of the people who are curious, but not before."

With calm, deliberate moves, she sighed and opened the book again, pretending to read. As if she'd not a care in the world. When in truth, she wanted to crawl back in bed and cover up with blankets in an attempt to avoid the world.

The tension between them ratcheted up a few notches but he let it go. Her heart tripled in speed as they circled for landing on the private strip. Night had fallen and she didn't even bother staring out of the window. She would see firsthand what awaited her out there soon enough. No need to expedite the information.

They taxied to a stop and she stood after the door had been opened. She didn't even have a bag to grip to give her hands something to do, for it had been taken from her. Three deep breaths and she followed Axel to the exit.

The entire area sat ablaze with light. She saw her family and her heart cried out in joy. She had missed them. There were also reporters and that was what kept her from running down the steps to the man people called king.

Axel put his hand on the small of her back and walked down beside her. She headed for the king first and stopped before him. Axel had halted a ways back.

"Hello, Father," she said in a soft voice.

"Zahra." His tone was ragged, and in seconds, he'd pulled her tight to his chest, hugging her as if he never wanted to let her go.

Yet she remained skeptical and kept her hug short. He drew back and stared at her, tears in his eyes.

"What's wrong?"

"I'm not sure how much emotion I'm supposed to show for your reporters. I wouldn't want to disappoint you my first day back."

Yes, bitter, but she'd been schooled on proper protocol for so long and given she was aware of her position in the kingdom—as a bargaining piece—she was suspicious at how much of his concern was real.

Self-disgust skated over his face and he waved a hand to his guards. "Get the reporters out of here. This is a private family moment."

His men didn't ask questions and soon the flashing lights had been removed, leaving only Axel there with her family. Her father hugged her once more and the tears threatened to escape her eyes as she held him tight this time.

As her mother enfolded her in her arms, Rally heard her father talking to Axel about how grateful he was to him for bringing her home.

It's not like he was the one who saved me.

She reunited with her siblings then was pulled back to her father's embrace. The place she used to feel the safest growing up. The faint scent of his tobacco and spice filled her nose and this time the tears did fall.

They escorted her into an SUV and she rode the way back to the palace tucked against her father's side. Once inside, she was whisked away from him and taken up to her room where her mother oversaw them preparing a bath for her.

She'd sunk below the hot water, her head against a rolled-up towel, her mother beside her.

"I'm so sorry for everything you went through, baby."

She cracked open one eye and angled her head to see her mother clearly. "You didn't bring my plane down, Mother."

"How did you survive? Where were you? What happened?"

She yawned and her mother shook her head.

"Never mind. We'll talk about it later. Right now, you need to relax in the bath. I'll have Jana attend you when you're finished."

"Thank you."

"You must be hungry. You're far too thin. I'll have the cook whip up some of your favorites." She pressed a kiss to her forehead and left Rally alone.

The heat seeped into her body and she found she was sinking as sleep snuck up on her. She held out as long as she could, and when she stood, Jana was right there with her thick robe. Tying the belt, she stared at the maid.

"Could you find me something two piece, long pants and sleeves if possible, please?"

"Yes, Your Highness." She curtsied and hurried off.

Rally stood before the mirror and stared at her reflection. Better than when she'd first made it out of South America but not quite back to where she had been prior to the entire trial.

She made a slow walk around the bathroom and her room. The items were beautifully crafted and yet for the life of her she wanted the simple furniture of Ethan's house. Hell, she wanted him. She longed to hear that deep voice with the southern accent speaking in her ear as he held her.

No lie, the sex was amazing, but she loved being held by him. He was the first person who made her feel important and as if she meant something to the one holding her.

"Here you go."

Rally turned to find her maid there, arms outstretched with a purple PJ set in them. "Thank you." She took the clothing.

"Did you need help?"

"No, I'm fine. Could you please go see if the food has been prepared? And if it's not been sent up yet, please ask for a cup of peppermint tea to be sent along with it. No sugar, just honey, please."

Another curtsey. "Right away, princess."

Alone, she dressed in a short time and felt a tiny bit better to have long sleeves covering the scarring on her legs and arms. The flannel may have been too warm for the time of year but she needed the extra protection. It wasn't the time for her to be dressed in the tiny lace negligees she had far too many of in the closet.

She'd curled up on a chaise when the door opened again, admitting Jana and a kitchen staff pushing a cart laden with more food than Rally would ever be able to eat on her own.

"Welcome home, Your Royal Highness."

The smile firmly affixed in place, she inclined her head. "Thank you."

When it was her and Jana, she gestured for the girl to sit with her.

Rally glanced over the offered spread. "That's a lot of food," she commented. "Help yourself, Jana."

"Princess?"

"Eat with me. I'm not eating in front of you, and if you want me to eat something, you'll have to join me."

"I couldn't."

"You can and you will. You don't eat, I don't eat." Lowball sure, but she didn't want to eat alone, much less in front of a girl who looked as if she could use a few good meals under her belt.

Rally fixed herself a small bowl of different delicacies and waited for Jana to grab some food. The girl took fruit. Tugging a soft blanket over her legs, Rally began eating.

She woke later when Jana recovered her with the blanket, long enough to smile at the girl then succumb to slumber once more. Tomorrow would be trying and right now, she wanted sleep, to forget where she was and to dream about where she longed to be.

The following mid-morning, she stepped through the door to meet the reporters waiting. She'd already met with her family and filled them in on her experience. She'd also had a sit-down with their public relations spokesman and had taken his advice on what to and what not to answer during the press conference.

Rally glided over the floor to her waiting seat and hoped she didn't muck this up. She also wished Ethan was beside her, offering the support only he could provide.

Chapter Thirteen

"Where are you, Ethan?"

"Den," he called out to his cousin. He curled his fingers around his beer and never took his eyes off the television screen.

"What are you doing?"

"Watching Rally's press conference. She's about to come in the room. So if you're going to be here, sit and be quiet."

Moments later, Beau occupied one of the other chairs, feet extended and a beer in hand.

Ethan's heart jumped when the doors opened to admit his princess. Her pantsuit was a stunning shade of sapphire. The jacket had an asymmetrical-wrap style that buttoned to the left with three gold buttons and accentuated her small waist. Her straight-leg pants fell to the tops of her feet. She wore heels and moved as if nothing on this earth could touch her. A simple gold pendant sat around her neck and three rings were on her fingers.

Her hair had been gathered upon her head in an elegant coif. Her father already sat but stood when she approached the table.

Ethan's eyes narrowed as the king pressed a kiss to his daughter's cheek. There wasn't any warmth in the man's gaze as he stared at his child, a child who'd been missing for years.

"She was right. She's nothing but a fucking commodity to that man," he growled.

Beauregard didn't reply.

As he watched them ply her with questions and heard her scripted responses, his gut soured. There was nothing of the passionate woman who'd shared his bed there. Not even a little bit. Aside from the looks, he stared at a different woman. She was polite but a bit reserved. Her words were all the correct ones yet he couldn't detect any emotion in them. There definitely wasn't any in her eyes.

"That's not Rally," he said.

"No it's not. This is the Princess Zahra you're looking at, Ethan. You can't forget that."

"What do you want me to do? Go back to Rolf and see if he can remove those thoughts from my memory banks? Because I'm not going to up and forget Rally. The woman who shared my bed and made me laugh. The one who saved my fucking life."

"I don't expect you to forget her but we all have a role to play and right now, she's playing hers. Which is that of a princess. She has to sit there and take those questions because she was told to. Even I can tell that she was coached on what to say and how little to reveal. She's even acting a bit hesitant."

"I'm never going to forgive Anabelle Lee," he snapped.

"That's between you two. I'm not getting in it. All I know is we know she made it home safe, hopefully her life will start to settle down."

Ethan shot a glare to his cousin. "You think I'm letting her stay there to be sold off by her father?"

"I think we have enough on our plate right now with trying to find Rolf."

"No more than you did while you still looked for me."

"That's different, you're family."

"And she's my family, Beau. I love her. I want her as my wife. I want to be the father of her children."

His cousin swore. "How do you propose doing that? You going to head over there and beg an audience with their king?"

"If that's what it takes. I may sneak in there and kidnap her."

"Christ, Masters is going to kill us."

Ethan sat forward. "Us?"

"You don't think I'm letting you go there alone, do you?" He leaned farther and rested his forearms on his thighs. "This isn't going to be easy."

"Somehow I think Grams would say anything worth a damn wouldn't be."

"I'll get us some plane tickets to go over there. We'll have to hump it in. We can't fly into that country."

"I'll be ready to go when you are."

Beau stood and glanced down at him. "Are you sure about this?"

"More than anything."

"Alrighty then, let's bring her home. Make plans to leave in two days so I can set up other arrangements while we're there. Just in case we need a contingency plan."

"We'll need one," Ethan said, getting to his feet. "We always do."

"It's called eternal optimism that we will one day not be in need of one."

Ethan snorted. "It's us, cuz. We'll need one."

"True enough. I'll see you in two, and Ethan… If you leave without me, I'll kick your ass to the point you will wish you were back in that hellhole."

"Noted."

Beau left and Ethan moved toward the flat screen on his wall. Rally still gave her interview but he didn't care to hear it. That wasn't where she belonged. She belonged with him. Here.

A short time later, he was on his way to Grams'. He parked by her old car then hopped down before striding up to the house.

Pushing his way in, he called out, "Grams?"

"In the living room, Ethan. The coffee should be ready. Bring it in, will you?"

He smiled. "Yes, ma'am." Putting the requested items on a tray, he also added the plate of cookies he spied.

Carrying it in the living room, he found Grams seated in her favorite rocker, quilting.

"You know you can use a machine to do that, Grams. I hear it goes much faster that way."

"I'm not in a rush. It's you young people who are always rushing around."

He put down the tray, poured her a mug of coffee and kissed her check when he gave it over to her.

"How'd you know I was going to come over?"

She clucked at him while he fixed his own drink and occupied a chair near her. The quilt had images of magnolias and other bright flowers intermixed with subtler and toned-down musical notes. The offsetting colors were both vibrant and cohesive.

"I raised you, Ethan Jackson. There's no one who knows you better."

She wasn't lying.

"That's gorgeous, Grams. Who's this for?"

"This is your sister's quilt."

"Why the music notes? She's not at all the least bit musically talented."

"Never you mind. Before you ask, your quilt is finished. Once I'm done with Anabelle Lee's, I'll work on Beauregard's. Have you made up with your sister yet?"

"No, ma'am, and I'm not going to. She took this too far this time, Grams."

"Took what too far? Protecting her brother who she thought had been taken from her forever?"

He didn't appreciate the reprimand from Grams but didn't comment on it. Instead, he took a drink of his coffee and smiled. Kenyan. The kind he liked. Anabelle Lee and Beau had their own favorites, so for her to have brewed this, she had expected him to show.

"That's not the point, Grams. She offered to send her home. Pushed her into leaving before she was ready."

"Not true. I saw her today on the press conference. She looked perfectly calm and collected."

A low rumble rose in his throat. "That's not Rally, Grams. That's the princess who's not supposed to make any waves."

"We each have roles to play in life, Ethan. Like it's mine to pretend you and Beau aren't planning to go get her back, or that Anabelle Lee will show up as well. We each have them and we fulfill them. In my case, it's because I can't stand to think what could or may happen to any of you. I pretend I don't know how dangerous your work is."

How the hell does she do this? Beau and I just came up with that today. He sipped some more coffee.

"We're not—"

"Do us both a favor, Ethan, and don't lie to me. We know you're going but it's not something we need to discuss further. It is a fact and is what it is. No different than you know your sister has your back even if you two are fighting like a couple of angry dogs with each other."

He shut his mouth. She was correct on that.

"Instead you can tell me when you will be by for dinner."

"I'll be here tonight, Grams."

"Very well. We will be eating at six-thirty."

"Yes, ma'am." He finished his coffee and got to his feet. After fixing his grandmother's refill, he took his mug out to the kitchen and washed it. As he was leaving, he ran into his sister who was walking in the door.

He stared at her then bypassed her without saying a word. Not even her heavy sigh got him to stop and turn around. He had things to do, a rescue to plan, a woman to recover and bring home.

* * * *

Rally stood overlooking the pool. The lights surrounding it were solar and the glow a soft amber one, but it did nothing for her. She used to love it out here. Now it bothered her.

"How are you doing?"

She started at her father's voice. Turning, she watched him appear from the darkness. She forced a smile.

"I'm fine, Father."

He reached out as if he were going to touch her face, yet allowed his arm to drop back to his side. "You know, there was a time when you called me Daddy."

"A lifetime ago." She faced the water again as he settled in beside her.

"Was it truly so long?"

"Before I learned I was nothing more than a commodity to you and your holdings."

He sucked in a sharp breath. Rally ignored the glare.

"You have a wayward tongue."

"Such a shame your friends weren't able to beat that out of me while they kept me there." She faced him.

"How could you imply I would have anything to do with your being taken?"

"Because the people who did had a saying that I saw daily. It never registered from where until I got back here. *Oderint dom netuant.*" She waited as the recognition sank in.

"Surely you were mistaken."

"Mistaken?" she gasped, heart rate tripling in speed. And lest it be forgotten a healthy dose of betrayal and heartbreak. "No, I'm pretty sure I can confidently recall the saying hanging on the wall near the *pole* I was tied to as I was threatened with rape and whipped repeatedly until I fell unconscious."

"It couldn't be," he stuttered, all of a sudden looking so much older than he had previously.

"Don't tell me you're going to try to convince me you had nothing to do with this now?"

"I didn't and I know you don't believe that but it's true. When you went missing, my life changed."

She snorted. "I'm sure it did."

"Not because I couldn't sell you off but because you were my baby. My youngest. The one who used to look up to me, and even as you got older, you kept me paying attention to the plight of others.

"Leah would have been here but she's off on maternity leave. She married and is having her second baby."

"I thought you would have fired her."

"No, she was the one you were closest to. I kept her around, in essence, so I could still be close to you."

God how she wanted to believe those words but she was beyond skeptical. "And the Latin?"

Her father picked up her hands and turned her toward him. "I swear to you on this entire kingdom and everything I have of value in the world, I was not behind it. I know who was now and I promise you they will pay."

He drew her close and hugged her. Rally didn't fight it, just wrapped her arms around him and cried. She allowed the tears to fall.

As the minutes passed, so did the years, until she was again the young girl who idolized her father. The child who would sneak into his throne room and play, waiting for him to arrive and play with her. The young girl who would slip him little notes in his packets of paperwork so he would have something to smile about during his day.

She could see his face the day she'd made him cookies herself, burned and barely edible, and taken them to him. He'd eaten not only one but two, just to see her smile. Then later on, taken her back to the kitchen where they'd made a batch together.

Rally drew back and kissed him on the cheek. "Thank you."

"You're my baby. It's not just my job to protect our holdings. It's my job to protect you as well. And I failed at that, but I won't again."

He walked her to her room and left her with another kiss. She waited all of three seconds after he'd vanished around the corner to go after him. They may not have been close all these years but she knew him and she wanted to know what he did.

Her father stopped by her sister's door. He pounded, and when it opened, he pushed his way in, slamming it shut behind him.

Rally continued on to the head of security's office. She knocked and stepped inside.

"Princess?" The head guard sat up straighter and snapped closed his laptop.

"I need access to the files."

He gave a small shake of his head. "Is there something specific I can pull up for you?"

"No. You can give me access and step aside."

He ran his gaze over her in a blatant and inappropriately familiar way. Rally narrowed her eyes.

"You have three seconds to oblige my request and I'll forget about the porn on your computer you were jacking off to instead of protecting my family. If you don't, then we will go see my father about it, as well as these looks you seem content to give me."

Her tone held the right amount of bitch for he stood and brought something up on the main computer before he held the chair for her. "I'll be over here if you need me."

"Thank you," she said, taking a seat.

When he sat, she typed in the phrase she'd given her father. The hits where it was mentioned popped up and she perused each one. The first five resulted in nothing for her. But the sixth one, it pulled up an image of the man she knew as Rolf.

She gasped and waved off the man's inquisitive glance in her direction. Next to Rolf was her sister, the one her father had gone to see. There wasn't anything romantic in the image between the two of them but it didn't matter to Rally.

Her sister knew the fucker who'd made her life hell. She sent it to the address she recalled Ethan using so he could get an identification on the man. Moving faster now, she went through the others and found some images of this man with Axel. Bile rose fast and almost escaped her mouth to spew all over the screen.

"Thank you," she stated, bolting for the door.

"You're welcome."

Destination in mind, she strode over the empty palace halls to her sister's suite of rooms. She didn't knock, just pulled them open and walked in.

"Neda," she called out. "Where are you?"

Her sister, the second oldest, shuffled into view. "What are you doing here? Is everything okay? Can I get you something?"

"Can the shit, sister. I know you set this thing up with Rolf. My question is why?"

Her sibling's smooth expression morphed into something ugly. "You brought it on yourself. All your protesting, your rallies for those who didn't have as much. You were a disgrace. You weren't supposed to be back without him."

"Without who?"

Neda's expression grew haughty. "I'm not telling you. I sold you, you know. Told him where you'd be and when."

Rally had no way of ignoring the fury that raced through her. "Told who?"

"You'll see tomorrow. He'll be here to marry you."

"I'm not marrying Axel."

"You will if you want him to live."

"Him? Him who?"

"Your boyfriend, Ethan Jackson."

Her heart plummeted. *How does she know about Ethan? I never gave out his name.* "I don't have a boyfriend. Nice try."

"We know the man who saved you. His name is Ethan Jackson. He wasn't supposed to escape but then neither were you."

"What did I ever do to you?"

"You were born. It was bad enough with the other kids, but when you came along, he took away my attention and gave it to *you.*"

"Blame the ones who created me. It's not my fault." She edged around back to the door, fully aware now her sister was batshit crazy.

"Father will have me punished, but that's okay because when my punishment is over, you'll still be married to Axel. And he has such plans for you."

"I'll never marry him."

"So you think." She pointed to the door. "Get out of my room."

Rally didn't argue with her. Her mind on Ethan, she scrambled to figure out a way to get a warning to him. He may not check his file that often and she had to alert him that trouble was on its way. Had to protect him and Grams.

She broke into a run and dashed up the corridor. In her room, she picked up her phone only to hesitate. *What if this is nothing more than a ploy?* Dropping the item, she ran for the security office once more and burst in.

"Sorry," she said, "I forgot to do one thing while I was here before."

The guard stood and backed away from the computer. She sat down and sent a message to an account, one she hoped was checked more often than not. Giving him the only warning she could provide without giving it all away.

Please let that be enough to sufficiently warn him and his family. She worried her lower lip and prayed she'd not just made a grievous error in regard to Ethan's life.

Chapter Fourteen

The hot, humid air smacked him in the face as the Jeep they were in careened over the bumpy landscape. He'd missed the thrum pumped into him from a mission and for a while there had been afraid he'd never experience it again.

Beside him in the back, Beau sat, chewing on a cheroot. The man didn't smoke but it had been a gift from one of the guards they'd passed along the way who'd been appreciative of the money slipped to him.

"What?"

"Just thinking how much your ass would hurt if Grams saw you with that thing hanging out of your mouth."

"Why do you think I only do this on continents she's not on?" Beau grinned, flashing white teeth against his tan skin. The man came off as being at home in his olive-drab BDUs and the black shirt. The weapons attached to him were part of him, not accessories. Currently, the man stared at his phone.

"What's going on?"

"Message from a girl."

"Seriously? Are you getting dates while we're on this mission?"

"First, she was looking for a follow-up date, which I don't do. And this happened way before we came here."

"You do know if we look at the picture beside the term manwhore it's you, right?"

Beau flashed his smile. "I give the women what they want. Nothing more, nothing less."

"Except commitment."

"True. I'm not one for that. I'll leave that to you."

"So long as it's with Rally, we're fine. You, however, stay away from her. I don't want your germs jumping off onto her."

Beau laughed and shoved his phone back in his pocket. Ethan didn't know how he did it. Personally, he wasn't comfortable being with all those women. Women talked and that could always end poorly for the guy.

Their ride slowed and they both readjusted their hold on the weapons.

"What's going on?" he hollered over the engine to the driver.

"We reached the end of the road. You'll have to go on foot from here."

They were standing by the time the Jeep came to a complete stop and both hopped out. Shaking hands, they thanked the driver.

"No problem at all. You sure you two want to do this alone?"

"I think it's better this way than rolling up to a palace with an army. The king may take exception to that."

"From what I hear of him, he'll take exception to this way as well. Not to mention the fact you touched his daughter."

Ethan looked at Beau.

"What? We're related. It's a viable assessment of what happened between the two of you."

"Some days I hate you," Ethan groused.

"I can live with that. Let's get out of sight in case people come to check on the engine. Thanks again for the ride, Sam. We appreciate it."

"You've got my number. Give a call if you need exfil."

"Don't fall asleep away from your radio. I have a feeling we'll need one," Beau said with a grin. "Excuse us why we literally go save the princess."

They dipped into the jungle and allowed it to swallow them up. As they moved in tandem, Ethan noticed the change flow over his cousin. He and his sister were both damn good at this job but Beauregard took it to a different level.

He didn't just move through a landscape, he became part of it. Hell, if he hadn't known the man was with him, he would have assumed himself to be alone. No trace or visual sighting of his cousin.

He didn't wonder where he'd gotten to—it was Beauregard's way, typical when he wasn't point. He would be around if needed—otherwise you would have to be part bloodhound or a predator to locate him.

After humping it through the heat and foliage, he reached for his water and took a bit of a break. As expected, Beau showed up. One second not there, the other he was.

"You holding up okay?"

Part of him wanted to be offended by the question but he couldn't afford to be. Beau asked for the sole reason of getting everyone out alive. And if he wasn't feeling up to it, that would mean that Beau would be watching not just Rally but also him.

"Tired, but otherwise fine."

Green eyes assessed him before his cousin nodded sharply once then slipped away without another word.

Ethan sat there for a few more moments, regulated his breathing and heart rate before standing, shouldering his bag and getting back on with his mission. When they stopped for the night, Beauregard didn't look the least bit put out while Ethan was wishing he could go for a long hot shower and sleep in his bed.

Too many nights in a small dark cell for him to like being away from the comforts of home. Those comforts he wasn't sure he'd ever take for granted again.

He caught an MRE from his cousin, tore open the pack and dug into the spaghetti. "What'd you get?"

"Beef stroganoff. Why, want to switch?"

"No, I'm good. Cold noodles are cold noodles."

"True." Beau crouched beside him for a few seconds then lowered his large frame all the way to the ground. "You don't miss this, do you?"

"I thought I did, but to be honest no. I don't. I pushed myself because I thought the thrill and the adrenaline were something I craved still in my life. Just so we're clear, it's not. I like doing the computer side of it, always have, that's no secret. But being out here... I don't know. It's not as welcoming as I'd hoped it would be."

"Nothing wrong with that. Theta needs you on the computers, perhaps even more than they need you out in the field."

"You trying to convince me to give up field work and take an office job?"

"I'm saying if you want to marry a princess, you should not be traveling around the world where your face will be known when you can appear to have a corporate job and still help protect our country and the world. But this way, you're home for dinner each night. Hell, you'd be able to work out of your house."

Sealing up his trash in a bag to contain the smell from wild animals, Ethan sucked the remnants off his thumb. "Tell me the truth. You're okay with me and Rally?"

"Not my place to comment on it one way or the other. You are happy with her, happier than I've ever seen you. For that reason alone, I'm for it. But I'm also no fool and I understand that for you and her to work, it won't be easy. You have to get her again and convince her to be with you outside of the palace. No way in hell Grams is okay with you coming over here to live."

Truth.

Ethan grunted before leaning against the thick trunk behind him. "You think Rally will have a hard time leaving this?"

"I'm saying for a woman who grew up in a palace, living in the woods in Georgia may be a bit more difficult than expected."

"But she was a prisoner for years in the jungle and…" Understanding hit him. Why in the hell would the woman want to be back in a place more similar to where she'd been held captive than in a palace where everything she would want was taken care of?

"Not saying she won't want to be with you but you need to be prepared for her not wanting to come back with you, Ethan."

"Point taken."

If only his sister could have been on the same page. He would have loved to have her support for this as well.

They settled down to sleep and Ethan woke to a sharp word from Beau. He sat up, reaching for his weapon when lights shone down on them, blinding him.

"Don't move." The words fell in a rough deep tone.

When the light moved and adjusted enough that he could see the man behind it, his heart stuttered a bit. This was none other than the man they had pegged as Axel Frost.

* * * *

Gazing across the ballroom, Rally sighed and tried to contain her boredom and hide her fear for Ethan and his family. She refused to show it—however her sister, the traitorous bitch, watched from across the massive ballroom. What her father was going to do to her sister, she hadn't any clue, but she was sure it would be something. Her father was staying a bit closer.

Unfortunately, that also meant guards were around her more, as was Axel. For whatever reason, he'd chosen to stick around as a personal guest of the king. As if her thoughts had summoned him, he strode into view, dressed in a black tuxedo with a deep purple cloth in the pocket.

He spoke with people as he passed them and she fought the urge to slink back into the shadows so he wouldn't spot her. It was too late when he smoothed his hand down the front of his silk tux and the cold, practiced smile she recognized well lifted his thin lips.

Damn.

The cameras followed him as he neared and she fixed her expression to the professional one the princess presented in public. The one that wouldn't offend her father or anyone in her family.

Not that she cared, but appearances must be kept.

"Good evening, Your Highness," Axel said with a sharp bow.

She inclined her head. "Mr. Frost."

"May I have the pleasure of your company for a stroll around the grounds?"

Lord help her, it was on the tip of her tongue to tell him not in a million years, but when her father turned to glance in her direction, she gave her agreement. The ballroom opened into a large labyrinth that people wandered into to spend time alone, and she wanted nothing to do there especially with this man.

"Exceptional," he said.

For a moment, they both stood there, not moving, until he remarked, "It is not for me to offer my arm."

Yeah, she knew that. So she offered her hand and he took it, setting it in the crook of his arm. She didn't want to touch him. Hell, she didn't want to be in the same room as him. Knowing that he somehow knew Ethan scared her beyond belief.

The man held his piece as they made their way around the interior. As he guided her through the open double doors, his grip tightened on her arm.

"You need to loosen your hold."

"Always so arrogant and presuming you're above everyone else."

"You don't comprehend how wrong you are about that, Mr. Frost. I've never thought myself better than others. Better than some, yes. And you would be one of them."

"I'm going to enjoy taming that mouth of yours. For whatever reason, you weren't delivered to me this last time but I have you now and you will become mine. I will have access to your father and you will pleasure me in ways I can only imagine at the moment."

"You seem to have a very high opinion of yourself, Mr. Frost."

"I know how to play to my strengths."

"Is that why you're working with the ones who kidnapped me and held me hostage for numerous years? Because you *know* how to play to your strengths?"

"Again, that wasn't supposed to happen. You were supposed to be delivered to me. I need to arrange a meeting with Millard about how that happened. He shouldn't have had you. Ethan, he could have and do whatever he wanted to. But you were mine. Are mine."

The possessiveness in that tone chilled the blood in her veins. With a haughty sniff, Rally shook her head. "I will never belong to you."

He nodded at the people they passed, giving them a smile. "You can tell yourself that but I will prove to you different. And when I come to your bed at night you will learn just how some things are to be."

"You mean that you like men in your bed?"

He stiffened and stutter-stepped. She laughed lightly, despite the amusement only being skin deep.

"You're not the only one who has their ear to the ground. You forget, Mr. Frost, I'm not the same as my other sisters and brothers who are content to stay in the palace and have their life handed to them on a silver platter or be catered to every second of the day."

He paused by the entrance to the labyrinth. "You don't know what you think you heard."

"Really? You hope I don't. Your proclivities don't scare me, Mr. Frost. I don't give a damn if you like boys or girls. Hell, the fact you want both. I know how you get off on administering pain, all of it. I've known since before you walked into my life and snowed my father into thinking you were something you're not even close to being. People out there talk, and while you may not have been able to fulfill your desires inside the palace, you surely went out to town and did a number on those people there. They don't forget and scars don't fade."

"You think you know what it's like to be in my bed?" He put his face close to hers. "You don't, but I promise you, you will."

The line of menace in his words should have scared her, and if she'd not gone through the hell she had in the rainforest, it probably would have. But she *had* gone through it and she *wasn't* a victim—she was a survivor. Fear had no place in her world.

"There isn't anything you could remotely do that would scare me. Not that this matters. My father isn't giving me to you."

He propelled her inside the first bit of the maze. "And why do you think that? Are you hoping your lover will come save you?" A diabolical grin lifted his thin lips. "He won't, you know. We have him as a prisoner."

Her heart thudded harder. Ethan was here? And a prisoner again?

"I don't have a lover—not that it's any of your business. It's because when I tell my father what you want to use me for, he will say no." *All right, I agree, this is a bold statement for me to make since I have no idea what my father will do.*

"Sure you will," he said with a sadistic smile. "Because if you don't do as I want you to, I'll have them kill not just Ethan but also his cousins and his grandmother."

"You keep talking about these people like I should know them. Are they people I've met in town?"

"You're good, princess, but trust me, I'm better. I'm actually having Ethan brought out here to where we're going so you can see I have him and I'm not bluffing."

To hell with it. "If that's the case, then I'm sure you are well aware how often I fucked him, spread my legs open for him and took his thick cock."

Axel's grip tightened on her arm. Tears she ignored sprang to her eyes.

"What's the problem?" she taunted. "Don't you want to hear how he made me scream his name? How many times I lost my voice because of him?"

"You will shut up if you know what's good for you," he growled. "You didn't sleep with him. You said you didn't even know him."

"You are the one determined to make me. Having known him, I figured I could just pad how well acquainted I am with this man."

"Being a princess isn't going to save you when I get a hold of you."

Unaware of where this confidence came from, she smiled what she hoped was an icy, patronizing smile. "You'll never get a hold of me. My father won't agree to it."

"I don't like this cocky attitude and will have fun beating it out of you."

"All these threats against the royal family *will* have repercussions, you know."

"No one will believe you, *Rally*."

Before her abduction, she would have been inclined to believe him, however. Now, while her interaction with her father hadn't been all that long, she hoped he was on her side. From his expression, he'd not known about the incident beforehand.

Ripping free of Axel's grip, she turned to face him in the muted light of the labyrinth. "What do you hope to gain from this?"

"From what? My façade? Marrying a princess, of course." He made the statement as if it were foolish of her even to question his motives.

Perhaps he was correct in that. She should have seen it coming. This man had been plotting for a long time.

"Why me? Seems that you and my older sister are more inclined to be on the same page, given she was in on this entire thing with you."

"We are compatible and I do foresee sex with her in the future, but you are the one people want to know about. You are the one who's in the public's eye, even more so now than before you were taken."

"Taken," she said with a huff. "Taken is what happens when someone takes you to dinner or to a movie. I was kidnapped, abducted, and held for years because you had some motive with one of my sisters."

Rally's voice had dropped low and vibrated with anger.

"How *dare* you minimalize what I experienced as if I was merely out for a few hours with friends?" She balled her hands into fists. "You arrogant bastard, do you have *any* idea what my life was like there? How it felt to be responsible for those lives, when if I was good and stayed they wouldn't kill another?" The gleam in his eyes told her all she ever wanted to know about this lowlife. "Of course it wouldn't matter to you, you're psychotic and certifiable. Nothing matters to you aside from your pleasure."

"I'm a lot of things, princess, but I'd be cautious with what you address me as."

"I don't have to address you as anything. You're beneath me, Mr. Frost. Always have been, *always* will be."

His thin lips curved up then dipped. The slow-moving blood within her was like ice. The malice in his gaze unlike anything she'd witnessed before. Even with Rolf.

She watched his miniscule hand gesture and followed the men who gave a sharp nod before slipping away. Her heart thudded hard within her chest as she had little doubt she was about to be reunited with the man who'd protected and loved her.

"Walk with me," Axel demanded, gripping hard on her arm again.

She didn't fight him, just fell into step. As usual, there were royal guards stationed along the route but she didn't ask any of them for help. If she could save Ethan, she needed to focus on that. Obviously, Axel wasn't the most stable of people.

"This is my wedding gift to you," he said. "I'm allowing you to say farewell to the man you made a whore of yourself with."

She ripped free of him and smacked him in the face. "I'm no whore. You want to use that title, go speak to my sister, but don't you dare call me one." Her anger soared freely through her body and she shook from the intensity of roiling emotions.

He reached for her but stopped. She angled her head and saw two guards had witnessed the exchange and were approaching.

"Tell them to stop."

His warning fell on deaf ears. She crossed her arms and glared at him. "Where is he?"

"He? I think you mean they?"

"Your Highness?" the guard asked as he approached.

"Mr. Frost spoke out of turn. Thank you for checking on me, I am okay now." A quick glance to Axel's face and she added, "If you don't mind waiting over there. We need to finish our private discussion."

Hell, she wasn't dumb enough to send them away completely. He knew it and wasn't pleased — she couldn't miss the anger on his face.

"Not smart, princess," he growled the moment they had their relative privacy once more.

"We both know you have men inside this palace, Mr. Frost, otherwise you wouldn't be this arrogant. Bring Ethan out and whoever else you have and let's get this over with."

"He's on his way. Are you so desperate to say your farewells?"

Her words fell away for two men strode into view, with two men behind them. Ethan and Beauregard were being brought to her location. Her heart slowed then tripled in speed.

Both men had dark circles under their eyes and some faded bruising on their faces. She ran a swift look over Beau then moved on to Ethan. Then she took her time, enjoying the way his pants hugged his lower body, the tightness of his T-shirt and the way his blue eyes watched her with a burning passion. A possessive one.

"Rally?"

"I'm fine," she replied instantly, understanding the question in his tone.

God, I've missed this man.

In that second, she understood what she'd read in those romance books and had seen in those movies. What true love was. She wanted to be with him, where didn't matter, just so long as they were together.

Chapter Fifteen

Ethan lost all moisture in his mouth. Sure, he'd been beaten and not exactly treated as a guest, but that wasn't why. Rally, in her dress, knocked his breath out. It hugged each of her curves like a lover, personal and intimate. Highlighting all she had to offer and yet leaving a bit for people to wonder.

Untouched.

That was what came to his mind when he glanced at her. Until he spied the man at her side who held her arm. The touch was unwanted, he could see that by her body language.

"Don't let him goad you."

Beau's deep voice filtered through the haze of rage surrounding him. He latched on to the advice and took several deep breaths. What they'd done to him for the short time he'd been held didn't come close to being enough that he wasn't ready to spring into action and kill that fucker with his bare hands.

Then again, when it came to Rally—*his* woman—Ethan was always ready to protect her.

They were directed off to the side, him, Beau, Rally, Axel, and the insufficient number of guards to protect him.

"Ethan Jackson."

He held the man's gaze. "Axel, I presume." Containing his desire to sneer at the man, he maintained his cool expression.

"I'd hoped Rolf would have killed you, but then I was also supposed to have her immediately."

"I'm sure it was a difficult time for you, fucking my sister while you waited to see if I would ever come home," Rally sneered, tone as warm as the Arctic during a blizzard.

"We have our entire lives to spend making up for lost time, baby," Axel said, not dropping Ethan's gaze.

"Fuck you."

Rally hung close to her snapping point. Whatever she'd had to deal with before they'd brought him and his cousin up from the dungeon had started the unraveling of her collected behavior.

"What is this, Axel?"

Ethan worked to contain himself. He'd been so focused on the fucker touching Rally, nothing else had mattered to him. Beau barely moved so he knew his cousin had seen the man attached to that deep voice approaching.

"Just some business I need to attend to, Your Highness."

The king. Rally's father. Ethan jerked his gaze to the new man in the group. He wasn't sure what to think about him but he seemed smaller than he had in the pictures. Not any less powerful, just smaller.

"Why are you conducting business at one of my functions? And why are you touching my daughter?"

Axel swallowed and let go of Rally.

"Keeping her safe. These are two of the men who had her prisoner."

Ethan opened his mouth to protest, saw Rally do the same thing, but the king interrupted his attempt.

"You have the men who abducted my daughter, and when I ask you about what you are doing, you state 'tending to some business'? This is my daughter, Mr. Frost. I will take these prisoners."

"I can handle it," he protested.

The king looked down his nose at Axel and Ethan saw him much larger now. Here was the arrogant ruler who didn't put up with any shit from anyone. "You speak as if you have any say as to what goes on here. It would do you wise to remember you are a guest in my home, not a member of the royal family or my staff."

Axel swallowed hard and dipped his head. "Apologies, my king, I was merely trying to keep you from having to deal with this during the party."

"Positive this is why my palace has cells, to have prisoners detained until *I* am ready to deal with them. Not until you feel it appropriate. How exactly is it you feel you know the best punishment to mete out to the men who kidnapped *my* daughter? You who aren't even of royal blood."

That last bit fell from his lips with such indignation Ethan almost felt sorry for the bastard. Christ, what had it been like for Rally growing up in this kind of environment? His childhood had been loving with Grams and his cousins. This gave a whole new meaning to cutthroat in his opinion.

"I was protecting her."

"Funny, that's what your friend said."

Ethan shared a look with Beau. Who was this friend? His fingers burned with the need to touch her. To make sure Rally was fine.

He heard a whistle that told him they weren't alone. He knew it was Anabelle Lee. Her signature sound. She'd come. Regardless of what happened between them, she was there for him now, when it mattered.

"What friend is that?" Axel questioned.

The king waved his hand. "This one."

Both Beau and Ethan sucked in a deep breath when they saw Carlos enter the little powwow. He glanced at them.

"This is like a family reunion," Carlos said with a sick smile. "Where's my ex-wife? I believe you call her sister, Ethan."

His eyes grew round. Was this man crazy?

"Oh, she didn't tell you? We weren't just dating. We were married." A shake of his head. "Then the bitch divorced me because she disagreed with how I spend my free time. But now is my chance to be reunited with her."

"Stay away from my sister," Ethan growled.

"Actually I'm thinking we're going to be a lot closer than we were before. See, being out here in the labyrinth is nice for more than one reason. But a main one is that the palace guards can't see anything."

"You will address me," the king snapped.

Carlos punched him, sending him to the ground. "Shut up."

Rally screamed and ran to her father, holding him as he lay there.

"Now where is she? I know she's here. I can feel her." Carlos looked about.

"Get over here, Rally," Axel demanded.

"Go to hell."

"Come here or I'll put a bullet in your father."

Ethan worked his bindings best he could. Just a bit more. The guards with the king were behind him and Beau. One of them pressed something into his hand and he took a deep breath at the feel of a pistol.

Rally stood, held her dress so she wouldn't drag it on the ground and walked over to the man who'd threatened her father. Ethan snarled low when Axel slammed his mouth over hers.

"I'm going to kill your family, Anabelle Lee, if you don't come out and show yourself."

"Take me instead of them," she said, appearing.

"Anabelle Lee, no," Ethan protested.

"This is my mess, Ethan. I have to clean it up." She moved before Carlos, hands out at her sides. Before they blinked she aimed a small derringer at Carlos and shot. But he managed to get out of the way and it grazed him. He tackled her and punched her. Tossing her over his shoulder, he shook his head.

"I have what I want. You're on your own, Axel." Carlos disappeared with his men and Anabelle Lee.

Axel glanced at them. "He may have spared your life but I won't."

Ethan and Beau lunged in opposite directions. Ethan's bindings snapped and he shot Axel dead center of his forehead. Beau got him in the chest. Blood sprayed all over Rally and she stood shaking.

Ethan ran to her, firing at the others as he moved. After tackling her to the ground, he used his body to cover hers, protect her.

Moments later they were surrounded by more of the king's men. All holding weapons on them.

The king stood and walked over to him. "Get off my daughter."

Ethan did, taking it as a good sign that he wasn't shot on sight. He assisted Rally up with his left hand, maintaining his hold on the pistol with his right.

"Come," the king said to her, beckoning.

Rally stood tall, as if she didn't have blood splattered on her clothes and skin. "They are not the enemy, Father. Let them go."

"You are standing up for these men?"

"Yes. They were not the ones who took me. They were the ones who saved me."

"Then we shall all go inside. You will need to relinquish your weapons, however."

He and Beau gave them over. They stood in silence as the king ordered his men to look for Carlos and the redheaded woman. Then they all went inside.

They waited in an ornately decorated room with eight guards. Ethan wiped off his hands and smiled.

"We're still alive."

Beau gestured to the men around them. "They don't look too pleased about it."

He shrugged. "Oh well."

The door opened and the king entered. Ethan glanced behind him for Rally. She wasn't there.

"She's not coming." The king walked around them. "The daughter of a king doesn't associate herself with the likes of you."

* * * *

Rally bit her tongue as she tried to keep her patience. Her father, however, continued droning on and on until she couldn't stand it any longer. She jumped up and slammed her hands on the table.

"Enough."

The king looked at her, as did the others present in the room.

"Mind yourself, Daughter."

"No, Father. Not this time. I want to know where Ethan and Beau are."

He waved a hand. "Leave us."

All but immediate family left.

"You see fit to check my business?"

"I see fit to check on my friends." She tugged on her sleeve, wishing it was one of Ethan's oversized shirts. "Where are they? You've kept me in the dark on that for a week. I want answers."

"And if I killed them?"

Her heart slowed. She lifted her chin and glared at him. "I would never forgive you."

"Who are they to you?"

"I told you."

"No, you said what they did for you, but I want to know who they are."

"People I care about."

"And you don't think they are being nice to you because of who you are?"

She clenched her fists and glared from him to her mother and back. "*They* were my friends first. They don't care about that. I'm Rally to them, not a princess."

"But you are a princess," her mother added.

"Then maybe I don't want to be one anymore," she yelled.

Her father approached her. "Leave us." He never took his eyes off her as the rest of the family did as he'd commanded. "You think you are in love with him."

"No," she said. "I know I am."

"You cannot marry a commoner. Much less an American, white male."

She rolled her eyes. "I love him." Rally took her father's hand in her own. "I want to be with him. In America."

"You don't want to live in all of this?"

"No, I never did. I wanted freedom and people to like me for me. I wanted you to look at me how you used to before you saw me as something that could gain you more in your reign. I'm not needed here. Please don't pretend otherwise. Ethan looks at me as if I'm his moon and stars. That's what I want."

"He's white."

"I know that. I don't care."

"You should be marrying a prince."

"He's *my* prince, Papa. He's all I want in the world." She squeezed his hand again. "Please."

* * * *

The house was as she recalled. Rally knocked then stepped back. Moments later, Ethan opened the door and stared at her. Blue gaze roving over her face as if he couldn't believe he was seeing her.

"Rally?"

Nerves fluttering uncontrollably, she nodded. "Hello, Ethan."

His expression cooled. "Your father told us you wanted nothing to do with me. What are you doing here?"

"He was wrong."

Ethan held her gaze. "About what?"

"Everything. I want everything to do with you, Ethan. I love you."

"Don't fuck with me, Rally. I can't take it."

She wrapped her arms around his neck. "I'd like to fuck you but I'm telling you the truth. I love you and if you will have me, I'd like to stay."

"What about being a princess?"

"I'm still one but I'm the youngest. Nobody will miss me."

"Did you run away from home?"

"No. I have Papa's blessing."

He held her tight, mouth to hers. "I love you, Rally." A tender kiss. "Welcome home."

He lifted her and she hooked her legs about his waist. As the door closed behind them, she knew this was exactly where she belonged.

* * * *

Somewhere on the Indian Ocean

"You heard about Axel Frost and Carlos, right?"

The man in the white linen suit nodded as he reached for another cigar. "I did. But what's the status on Carlos? I heard he was still alive. I know Axel is dead. What about Carlos and the crazy militant, what was his name, Thomas?"

He had no doubt what the man's name was. Just liked to pretend he knew less than he did.

The man in the room with him shook his head. "Last I knew about Carlos was he had taken off with his ex-wife. He was injured but she was with him. Axel took two double taps. One in his chest and one in his head.

He's not going to come back from that, no matter how slick he's been in the past."

"No problem, he was getting to be a handful anyway. Plus, he dared touch what was mine." He cupped a hand along the young man's face who lay naked on the settee. "That was something I would have killed him for if he'd not met his unfortunate end this way."

"And the one known as Rolf?"

"Consider him dead for the time being. He's been rewired for a new assignment. These Jackson family members are getting to be a bit much so I've tasked him with something else. He had to go pick up an attachment."

"And the planes that we're dropping from the sky?"

Anger sparked in his mind and it was a struggle to keep it contained. This wasn't a 'we' operation. It was *his.* "Oh, that stops now. We needed to make sure we could do them and ensure that no one could figure out how it was happening. That is put on hold until I'm ready to drop a few more."

"Everything that we've been doing for the past few years is, what, just stopped for now?"

He snipped the end of his cigar and nodded as he circled to the man who dared question him. "Yes. And do you want to know why?"

"I would, yes."

"Give me your hand," he commanded.

The man watched him with questions in his brown gaze but complied. With the hand in his, he smoothed his thumb over the back of it, taking note of the light dusting of hair.

"See, the reason is because it's my money, my operation and my *fucking decision* on what happens around here."

Before the questioner could move and tug his hand free, the one with the cigar cutter took a finger off at the first knuckle, ignoring the screams of pain and the blood flowing.

"Never question me again. Paulo, go get him looked at and have someone come in here and clean this up after they bring me another suit. I think I have some splatter on this one."

His boy rose and slid from the room without even thinking of putting on any clothing. Well, perhaps he thought about it but he didn't act on it. Paulo knew he wasn't supposed to wear clothing in his house.

It didn't take his naked house boy long to bring a few people to drag away the whining man who acted as if it was his dick that had been snipped off instead of part of his finger. After he'd changed into a fresh linen suit, he stepped into another room where another man awaited him.

"Rolf."

"Sir."

"I am sorry it didn't work out for you and the princess in the rainforest."

Rolf shrugged. "I want a go at the sister. I will have to remind Carlos he owes me a few favors and have him turn her over to me."

"I don't understand your pleasure from that but whatever makes you happy, brother."

His paternal twin smiled. "I like discovering how much pain people can withstand."

"Is the place in Montana ready?"

"Yes, made to your specifications. I even put in a heated room so your little bitch can be naked and not lose anything vital during the winter chill."

"Are you jealous, brother?" He walked to his sibling and canted his head to the side.

"No. I don't see what the fun is in being with a young boy. I like my partners to have experience. Otherwise you're teaching and training all the time. I don't have time for that."

"To each their own. Mother used to say that."

"She was an insane bitch who said lots of things. I don't think she is worth quoting."

"Be nice, Rolf. Stay for dinner. We have some other things to catch up on and plan. I'm not done with the Jackson family yet and I want you to hear what I have in store for them."

Rolf smiled, displaying the sadistic smile not seen since his last interaction with Ethan Jackson. The siblings sat and waited for the drinks to be poured before the conversation began on what was going to come for the Jackson crew.

About the Author

Aliyah Burke is an avid reader and is never far from pen and paper (or the computer). She is married to a career military man, and they have a German Shepherd, two Borzois, and a DSH cat. Her days are spent sharing her time between work, writing, and dog training.

Aliyah loves to hear from readers.

You can find her contact information, website details and author profile page at http://www.totallybound.com.

TOTALLY
BOUND

Home of Erotic Romance

www.ingramcontent.com/pod-product-compliance
Lightning Source LLC
Chambersburg PA
CBHW020425180626
46812CB00003B/1148